I0819561

MORSEL

MORSEL

CARTER KEANE

NIGHTFIRE

TOR PUBLISHING GROUP
NEW YORK

This is a work of fiction. All of the names, characters, organizations, places, and events portrayed in this work are either products of the author's imagination or used fictitiously.

MORSEL

Interior art by Shutterstock

A Nightfire Book
Published by Tom Doherty Associates / Tor Publishing Group
120 Broadway
New York, NY 10271

www.torpublishinggroup.com

Nightfire™ is a trademark of Macmillan Publishing Group, LLC.

EU Representative: Macmillan Publishers Ireland Ltd, 1st Floor, The Liffey Trust Centre, 117–126 Sheriff Street Upper, Dublin 1, D01 YC43

The Library of Congress Cataloging-in-Publication Data is available upon request.

ISBN 978-1-250-39245-9 (hardcover)
ISBN 978-1-250-39246-6 (ebook)

First Edition: 2026

Printed in the United States of America

10 9 8 7 6 5 4 3 2 1

To Olivia, for doing the hard work of keeping me out of the woods

This sentence is a stalling tactic so that audiobook listeners who prefer to rawdog their way through literature have time to put down the mug they were washing, dry their hands, and urgently skip forward to avoid even the barest hint of what's speeding down the pike at them. If you are reading this in textual form and do not want to see trigger warnings but have yet to turn the page, I cannot help you. This is a choice you, a sentient being, are making.

Within these pages you will find depictions of violence (both graphic and structural), gore, covert drugging, a brief mention of transphobia, hallucinations, and discussions of both parental sickness/death and animal harm/death (the dog makes it out okay, I promise).

There are likely other triggers in this book that are less general and more specific to your lived experience (those with entomophobia may have a difficult time). My sincere hope is that you're able to identify these triggers yourself, put the book down, and have a good rest of your day.

MORSEL

Mom 3:23 pm: are you staying late today?

Lou 3:31 pm: yeah have to finish a report

Mom 3:34 pm: ok

Mom 3:42 pm: you work too hard

Lou 3:47 pm: -_(ツ)_/-

Mom 3:48 pm: i'm serious. it's not good for you. the more you give the more they take.

Lou 3:50 pm: What else am i supposed to do? Literally what's the alternative because I don't see it.

Mom 4:02 pm: idk

Mom 4:02 pm: i just wish you didn't have to sacrifice so much

Lou 4:05 pm: I know. It'll be worth it eventually. Just have to get through it.

Mom 4:10 pm: yeah

Mom 4:11 pm: i'm going to bed early. theres carryout in the fridge when you get home

Lou 4:27 pm: thanks! night

Text conversation, March 14, 2019

CHAPTER 1

Year of the cicada they're calling it.

Millions of them in the trees, littering the ground, boiling black spots on the hood of my car. The number you can see is most definitely outweighed by those you can't—the bodies that, after crawling up from their holes deep in the earth, have been trapped underneath by sidewalks, newly laid asphalt, sparkling development killing insects like a sheet of ice kills a drowning man.

It's a good image. I'd illustrate the first few panels in soft pastel with colors as bright and warm as the world they're working to reenter. The last frame—their bodies piling up below concrete—would be grayscale. Some of the digital ink smeared to give the impression of charcoal, but not the texture.

They're everywhere, and now there's one in the café thumping against the big bay window in a desperate bid to escape.

"Dude, get it," Emma says. "Squash it or something before a customer walks in."

Emma and I are the only two in Roasted!, which is her current place of employment and my lunchtime respite from my coworkers. The café is situated in Downtown Columbus. That means a bro with a two-hundred-dollar haircut or a WASPy product manager could pop in at any moment to make her life hell.

They're such slow, clunky things when they're not flying. The cicada's wings are translucent lattice bound by thin lines of orange-brown. In the right light the sheerness flashes cool-toned colors like hunter green, wet-earth brown. It's easy to cup it in my hands and hold it safe in the dome of my fingers. A shiver licks at my neck when its wings tickle my palms. I feel the crack of its exoskeleton against my skin like a premonition. Wouldn't take much. Just a little pressure—the pressing of skin on skin.

"Lou."

"Right, sorry," I say. "One sec."

Outside, Downtown Columbus is hot and humid. I hold my cupped hands out in front of me. Schrödinger's cicada. Will it be insectoid mush when I open my hands?

I open my hands to find it hale and whole. It lingers on the meaty rise where thumb meets palm, fluttering. A beat. Another. And then with a crinkle of lattice wings moving, it becomes nothing but a black dot speeding through the air.

"Thank you," Emma says when I get back inside. "I don't know what it is about Thursdays. One guy had me remake his frappe, like, three times."

"You want me to fight him?"

Emma grins and I feel like latte foam inside. This is exactly what I needed before my meeting with Ellis. It looms over me—inescapable and catastrophic—but at least now there's some sunshine in the mix.

"I don't know. He was pretty big."

"I got muscles. Look." I flex my biceps for her, and she rolls her eyes.

"Let's go over it again, okay?"

Roasted! smells like warm yeast and freshly ground coffee. Just walking in causes my chest to unwind and my shoulders to lower. At the mention of the probably-getting-fired script we've been workshopping, my insides wind back up and compress themselves into a hard little ball that sits leaden in my gut.

"'This job means the world to me.'" I put on a normal, not-forced-at-all smile on my face. "'You took a chance on me when no one else would. I can't begin to tell you how much I appreciate that.'"

The smile is not coming across as I intended based on the look Emma is giving me over the steamer. Possibly it is not coming across as human, at all. I put a little more force behind it and continue.

"'My performance has not been up to my standards. I want to change that. I am *committed* to changing that. When my mom got sick, you were all so understanding—'"

"Don't mention that," she says quickly. Her face is pained like the mention of my mom at all is enough to hurt. It's enough to hurt me, that's for sure. "He might act like he cares about that, he might even feel like he *does* care, but at the end of the day you doing bad work fucks with his money. That's what matters. Focus on that."

I unclench the bear trap of my jaw and try again. "'I know everyone's personal life impacts their work sometimes, but that's not an excuse. I'm ready to be the employee you deserve. I'm ready to do whatever it takes to be better.'"

"That's good! That's great!" She puts my extra-dirty iced chai at the end of the counter. "If he lets you stay you can unionize your coworkers."

I laugh. Emma is doing her master's in labor studies, which means she's deeply enthusiastic about radicalizing working people into collective action. As much as I agree, I'm too tired to even think about trying.

Emma giving her union-or-bust elevator pitch to Arden and Jena would be fun to watch, though. Both are multi-level marketing girlboss girlies till the day they die. Just as Emma pitched solidarity, Arden would launch into her speech on effective altruism as the only solution to saving the world. A weird ouroboros eating its own tail is born.

I stare into the cinnamon Emma sprinkled on my drink. I've never been into astrology or tarot or whatever, but maybe if I look at the speckles for long enough, I'll be able to foretell the perfect combination of words that glazes over every fuckup I've ever made at this job.

The line in my script about Ellis being understanding isn't a lie. He told me to take an additional week off when my mom first got sick. His mantra from the last two months has been, "Perfectly understandable. Do what you need to do."

And yeah, sure, those are the words that come out of his mouth, but that's not what his face says. That's not what the tense silences when I walk into a room where I was clearly the subject of conversation mean.

"Okay. Time to get fired by the hottest man I currently know."

Emma snorts. "First, he is not that hot. Second, you've got this. Confidence of a mediocre white man, Lou!"

▾ ▾ ▾

Arden and Jena are sitting at the lunch table when I walk in to deposit my drink in the fridge. I do my best to smile at them with both my mouth and my eyes. Emma said I'm getting better. I do not believe her, though I appreciate the support.

"Hey!" Arden says. Her smile doesn't reach her eyes either, but her teeth are so white it's easy not to notice. She's only ever at the office one or two days a week. Both commission and working from home are privileges of seniority. And it only took fifteen years of being the biggest suck-up known to humankind.

"Come sit with us. We can chitchat."

"Oh, thank you, but I have a meeting with Ellis."

She pauses. Her smile takes on the quality of a no-loitering sign—all confidence and no reason. That's not very charitable, I know. In my defense, the last time I tried to be charitable they conned me into a weekend MLM seminar that cost almost an entire paycheck.

The two main tenets of Ascent—the personal-development and self-help multi-level marketing scheme both Arden and Jena are constantly hustling—are that (1) only you can control your own life, and (2) only through a mindset shift toward abundance will you be able to save yourself and in turn save the world.

The secret third tenet is that, of course, Ascent alone can teach you to unlock that super-duper special mindset that'll propel you to success and happiness.

I didn't know this before I registered for the Ascent Discovery Weekend. Arden and Jena pitched it as taking control, making a difference, being the master of your universe, cracking that defensive outer shell to reveal the authentic you inside, etc.

Arden herself was one of the opening speeches on the first day. She has seniority there too, apparently.

"Victimhood is your shelter," she'd said, a giant live projection of her face on the screen behind her. "It's a second skin formed to protect against being accountable for your life. Shedding that skin will open you up to abundance. It's only through this abundance that we'll be able to change ourselves and through that, change the world."

I did not feel empowered after. All it did was make me feel poor.

"That's okay," Arden says. "How about after? Frank talk: You never hang with us anymore. You can talk about your dog. We love your Riley stories."

"Ripley," I correct her. They don't. To them, the only dog worth having is a goldendoodle with a two thousand dollar price tag. Definitely not a pit bull from a county shelter like Ripley.

The words "no thank you" are again on the tip of my tongue when I remember Emma's advice. "Be nice. Socialize. Make sure they see you being a team player. Bosses love that shit."

"Sure. If you're still here when we're done, I'll join."

"No backsies," Jena says.

She's the Theater Star Beta to Arden's Girlboss Alpha and consequently gets a side glare from Arden for her sheer audacity to . . . speak? Exist? I flee the break room before I can witness whatever passive-aggressive dressing down Arden's about to unleash.

I'm looking at my phone and not watching where I'm going when I run smack into a broad, immovable object. Large hands cup my elbows. For a brief, ecstatic moment I'm flush against a chest that smells like pine and campfire smoke.

"Whoa there."

The immovable object is a man—Ellis Katsaros. Partner at the Katsaros and Curie Company.

Need an abandoned mall appraised for an impending demolishment or a tract of land in the middle of absolute nowhere assessed for auction? Want a real estate agent for your multi-multi-million-dollar mansion? Katsaros and Curie have got you covered.

His smile is sly. There are crinkles around his eyes. His

hair and beard are black, with faint impressions of silver. His skin is olive-dark. A nose that could have been chiseled from a Greek bust sits in the middle of his face.

I step back. His hands slip from my elbows and immediately I want him to put them back. Even better around my wrists, or if I'm lucky my throat. I'm so distracted by my face flushing hot with blood and poorly timed lust that I completely miss the words he's just spoken to me.

His eyebrows quirk. He's amused. He thinks *I'm* amusing. Not sure if that's a good thing or not.

He repeats himself. "Are you okay? Didn't jostle you too bad?"

"Oh. No, I'm fine. Sorry. I wasn't paying attention."

"I'm glad to hear it. Why don't you pop into my office. I'll be right there."

With that, he's striding away like his hands cupping my elbows didn't just make me shiver from the top of my head to the tips of my toes.

It might be time for the nuclear option: Tinder. Better that than fantasizing about an unattainable man who is (1) my *boss* and (2) at least fifteen years my senior.

I sit in the chair across from his desk, which is a mess of crinkled papers, legal pads filled with scrawled writing, and an array of colored manila folders. My hands are sweaty. I stick them under my thighs, then think twice and lay them neatly on my lap. I used to be better at this. Slipping into the costume of a well-behaved and professionally hungry young woman used to be easy.

I learned everyone's name, wore a bra with an underwire

and concealer every day, took my lunch at the table, and made conversation. *I made an effort.*

The only true, consistent effort I've made in the last two months is the daily one of getting out of bed, trying not to think about the closed door at the other end of the house, and taking Ripley on a walk. I love those walks.

We start just as the sun is about to rise. By the time we're done meandering through the broken asphalt streets, the entire trailer park is painted burnished orange and Starburst pink. My mom used to be able to go on those walks with me. She stopped being able to go at the same time I stopped being able to make an effort in the office.

Confidence of a mediocre white man, I remind myself.

Ellis walks in with a mug in each hand. One he sets down in front of me. It's the most recent weird wellness tea Jena bought because she saw someone on Instagram say it "balances your hormones and clears toxins." I asked which of the more than fifty hormones present in the human body it balances. She didn't talk to me for the rest of the day. The second mug joins the water glass and K&C-themed thermos by his computer.

There's a joke about him being a beverage hoarder in there somewhere. I do not make it because I am a Professional who Loves to Make an Effort. I take a sip from the drink because I am a Team Player Who is Easy to Get Along With.

"Not a tea person?" Ellis asks when I grimace.

"No, I love . . . leaves."

And pseudoscience.

He leans back in his chair and fixes his gaze on me. The weight of his eyes makes me feel small. Like he could cup me in his hands and there'd be nothing I could do about it. He's tall. Six feet and a few. I think he could hold me down without much effort at all. Alluring.

"I think you know why I wanted to have this talk."

"I do. This job means the world to me. It's important to me to do good work, and I haven't lately. I apologize. I know that sometimes people's personal lives impact their work, but that's no excuse. I'm ready to be the employee I was when I started. I promise if you give me another chance, I'll be the most dedicated employee you have."

He hums. "I was so impressed with your tenacity when you first joined our family. When your circumstances aren't preoccupying you so much, you do excellent work. Don't you agree?"

My circumstances.

Is that what you call it when the mortality of the person who *made* you is laid bare? He's technically right. I'm preoccupied with the possibility of losing my mom. I'm preoccupied with being the sole breadwinner responsible for our rent, for our utilities, for my student loans, my mom's bills, all on a $35,000 salary. I'll stop being so preoccupied when she dies. Is that what he wants?

There is a chant in my head, *don't hurt him, don't hurt him, don't hurt him*. It runs in time with the chant telling me I should. Both thump in time with my heartbeat. It would feel good. It would feel good to surprise him with pain.

I smile and think of piranhas gnawing through flesh with razor teeth.

"I know how difficult this has been for everyone. I apologize. I'm lucky to be here, and I want to do my best."

I *am* lucky to be here. After graduation, it took a year of constant applications, interviews, third shifts at Taco Bell, and crying in my childhood bedroom each time I got a politely worded "go fuck yourself, we're hiring someone else" email. Every day my mom got older and that much closer to having a heart attack from the energy drinks she buys to work twelve-hour shifts before I ever got the chance to take care of her like she took care of me.

Ellis hiring me was like a ray of bright light into a dim world. It didn't matter that I hated every word of description of every office building and property dimension and zoning regulation that I wrote. I'd succeeded in acquiring an Office Job—which was something my mom and her STNA (State-Tested Nursing Assistant) friends talked about like a stranded swimmer would dream of a life raft. Surely I'd finally be able to repay my mom for the years of constant struggle that was providing for the both of us.

I itch to wipe my damp palms on my pants, to get up and pace, to grip Ellis's dark, curly hair and shake him until he understands what I'm feeling.

He leans forward like he's about to pass along a secret. In the warmth of his office, it feels intimate. The hook through my cheek pulls and I can't help but mirror the motion just a little.

"I'm going to be real with you for a second. You probably

think this"—he gestures to the building around us—"is just another part of a capitalistic hellscape. I'm just some boss looking out for my bottom line. In some ways I am. I want to keep this place running. I want to pay my employees. That takes money. Profit. Which means that when someone's cutting into my bottom line—"

He makes a neck-slicing motion with his thumb.

"I don't want to be that person because I'm *not* that person. I like you, Lou. Do you know how long it's been since there was someone in the office who could make me laugh? Do you think I don't know how you're reacting is normal? Someone you love is hurting. When my dad died . . . I was a mess. I felt like he had so much more to teach me. It's been eighteen years and I still feel that way."

He pauses and looks at a picture on the wall of four pale, white men with serious expressions standing together in a wooded setting. Surveyor equipment and a few walking canes rest against what looks to be a large box or crate in the middle of the four. A handwritten label that's been yellowed by time reads *Witten Collieries Co. Mine #3—Scioto County, Ohio.*

Ellis is very proud of the story. I know because he tells it at every company event I've ever attended.

His great-great-grandad was born in New York. When he was twenty-two, he decided to work his way out west. Through a series of anecdotes that Ellis tells with bright eyes and a smile, he ended up in southern Ohio working in a coal mine.

There was a mine collapse when the coal baron himself,

his business associates, and for some reason his daughter were touring the operation. Ellis's great-great-grandad saved the baron and his daughter (none of the associates, though, unfortunately). His great-great-grandad and the daughter subsequently married. The stories never touched on whether it was for love or for a reward.

Ellis's mother was attending The Ohio State University for an English degree when she met George Katsaros, a geology student, at an anti-war rally. He always makes sure to mention *that* one was for love.

The rest is history as told by the mouth of a millionaire commercial real estate appraiser who turned his back on the family business of devastating the earth to become a conservationist.

"They were so surprised when I stepped away," he'll say, grinning. "It's not *my* fault they raised an activist."

It's not like I don't believe him about his great-great-grandfather's rags-to-riches story. It's just that my mom told me our family was given a plot in the Black Forest when our ancestor saved a Russian duke from a bear. I did a DNA test, and we're almost entirely Welsh. Grain of salt is all I'm saying.

"The point is that I understand," he continues. "I *want* you here."

I don't know what's wrong with me—I just know there is a problem, because him telling me I'm wanted inspires a burbling, bubbling, just-about-to-cry feeling in my chest and behind my eyes.

"I *want* to be here."

If I can't make this work, if I can't keep moving up the corporate ladder until I get to an altitude that allows me to breathe, then what was the point? What was the point of my mom overworking herself until she got an ulcer to help me with college tuition? What was the point of coming in early and staying late or going to the ridiculous Ascent training that Arden badgered me about for months? I need to be here. There *has* to be a point.

He leans forward. "Here's what I'm thinking. You know about the donated charity work I do, right? We provide pre-inspections and appraisals for conservation groups free of charge. I want to put you on these jobs. It's a lot of driving, but it's low effort. The reports are simple. The inspection is nothing more than taking a few pictures of trees and fields. It's technically easy, but ultimately important work. It needs to get done, and the mountains wait for no man. Or woman."

He's said this before. Gone on rants about undying heaps of rock and earth sitting prone at Ohio's southernmost border. Something in my face—or maybe nothing concerning me at all—inspires him to go on another.

"Did you know Appalachia is one of the oldest mountain ranges in the world?"

Passion lights up his face. I could reach out to wrap the curls of his hair around my finger. I could pull down sharply and then he'd know exactly how I like it.

There is a goblin living in the back of my brain. He sits in the dark with letters strewn around his knobby knees. He plucks at them with grimy fingers and arranges them into suggestions spoken like orders. He's the one who was chanting for me to hurt Ellis. Sometimes, I don't stop myself from listening.

What would he do if you leaned into him? the goblin wondered a few days ago when we shared the elevator. *What would he do if you leaned into him, then crushed his nose with the back of your skull? Would his blood be warm? You should find out.*

I didn't. But I wanted to.

"You take a walk in Ohio's 'hills,' you're walking on six hundred million years of shifting earth. Those mountains are older than bones, Lou."

His voice is deep. I want to draw what he's just described. Ink and pen. A figure huddled under trees—in the distance, hills made of blood and bone. He's looking at me with his eyebrows creased, like he's thinking hard about something. I want him to think about me.

As a trainee, I've been relegated to walking through dusty warehouses and rotting strip malls to write down measurements and take pictures of concrete destined to be torn down. Driving to the middle of nowhere where I don't have to talk to anyone or measure anything and just take pictures of trees sounds like one hell of an incentive. I tell him exactly that.

His eyes crinkle like I've just said something delightful. "I'm not trying to *incentivize* you."

The way he says the word makes my chest feel tight and hot. Is this how you get a daddy kink? I think probably yes.

"The first one would be tomorrow. The McLaren property.

Sounds like enough of a breather for you to get your legs back under you, right?"

The goblin whispers, *He's asking if it's enough time for your mom to kick the bucket and you to get over it.*

I ignore the way my heart is thumping and tell the goblin to shut the fuck up.

"Yes. Absolutely. I won't let you down, I promise."

"I know you won't, kiddo."

Any other man and that word would drip with condescension. Because it's Ellis, it makes me flush. When he hands me a folder with an address, property plat, and aerial inside, I hold the folder in my hands and think, *Maybe things will be okay after all.*

CHAPTER 2

if I don't text later bigfoot got me

emailed you the address

Emma is gonna be so annoyed when she gets my text. I don't think Bigfoot lives in Lawrence County, Ohio. But if he does and he's got a hankering for girl-adjacent flesh, it never hurts to be safe.

Last night, Emma's face got all screwed up like she'd just sucked a spoiled lemon when I told her Ellis's offer.

We'd been sitting on her couch. There was some horrible movie on the TV, and Ripley had her head on my lap. When she motioned with her hand, her beer almost sloshed out of the clear glass she'd poured it into.

"I'm glad you get to keep your job. It also sounds like he knows you're desperate and won't complain when he gives you shit work. Do you get commission on these projects?"

"They're pro bono," I say. "And I'm not at that level yet."

"Uh-huh. So you don't get paid *and* your chances of being axe-murdered go up significantly? I don't know, Lou."

Explaining that the potential danger of trusting Ellis's word is nothing compared to the danger of losing this job feels too big. There's no *time* to find something else. I couldn't go from square one in some new company that wanted to start me out at entry level all over again.

Emma's parents are upper middle class. They'll retire when they hit sixty-five. Their lives were planned out for comfort. My mom's life had an invisible ticking timer counting down to the day she had a medical emergency bad enough she couldn't work anymore.

My mom didn't have anyone else. She'd *never* had anyone else. It had to be me. If I think about it too much—about how she was born to parents who didn't want her and into a world that took little bites out of her body and mind every single day in exchange for the ability to pay rent—I can't move with how it weighs me down.

I had to get to a place where I could support both of us before the timer hit zero—even if it meant keeping a job that might be physically sucking my soul out through my pores.

Emma couldn't understand, so I didn't explain it, and then we drank until I was drunk enough to pass out on her couch. When I woke up this morning, she shoved her phone in my face. It was open to the podcast episode she'd listened to as she fell asleep, about some guy going missing years ago in vaguely the same area where I'd be.

"People go missing all the time," I said, my throat parched

and voice rough. "Especially in, like, parks and woods and whatever."

"That's literally the point!"

"So, what, you're never going camping again? 'Cause I guarantee someone died in whatever national park you pick. If you look for death you'll find it. I'll be careful, okay?"

She glared at me, then rolled her eyes and went back to getting ready for classes. Me sending her my location was an easy compromise so that she wouldn't worry so much. Despite that, she still tried to insist on giving me the hide-a-key her dad had installed behind her license plate.

"For your spare in case you lose your keys in the *fucking forest*!"

I declined and told her I'd keep them deep in my backpack the whole time.

Ripley stands in the passenger seat, stretches, then sits back down. I crack the windows, then turn off the car and slide into the muggy heat of late-August Ohio. The inside of the car is cold as tits from the AC. Ripley should be fine for the couple minutes it takes me to pee.

Outside, the heat is an oil slick that slides over my skin to settle at the base of my spine. I blow a line of too-long bang out of my eyes, then swipe my card at the pump. I need a haircut. Or scissors. Maybe a knife.

No less than three cicadas land on my pant leg as I walk to the store. I smile vaguely at the attendant on my way to the restroom. The women's is locked, so I slip into the men's. If I was going to pick a gendered restroom based on something other than availability, it'd be the one made for individuals who identify as the human-shaped approximation of a void. The Mariana Trench of people. Other people just say agender, but that's honestly just not as accurate.

My phone starts buzzing while I'm buttoning up my jeans. I catch it just as it's about to take a dive out of my pocket and onto the questionable floor.

"Hello?"

"Lou-Lou!" Ellis's cheerful voice fills my ear. A smile pulls my lips up in answer.

I like my name just as it is. Modifications feel like an insult nine times out of ten. I'm not sure why, but with him it just feels like he's trying to make me laugh.

I'm met with the glare of the man waiting outside when I open the bathroom door. His expression takes on a disgusted edge when he sees I'm not a cis man. This is when I do something I really shouldn't: I wink.

Lou, I can hear Emma sigh

Nice one. The goblin laughs.

He blocks my path. Looms. "You think you're funny?"

"Yeah. Do you think *you're* funny?"

Red spots bloom on his cheeks. He's wearing khaki shorts and has an assembly-line Great Clips haircut. This man looks exactly like every white middle-aged father in every sitcom that's ever been made.

The expression goes that all men are dogs. In reality, it's not just men, it's most people. Showing fear is what gets you bit. So I stand my ground, look him in the eye, and, like dogs and most people do, he backs down.

He sneers and spits, "Bitch," before walking away.

I breathe out long, then swallow to wet the desert my mouth has become. I put the phone back to my ear and am met with the tail end of Ellis saying, "Hellooooooo?"

"Hey! Sorry. I'm back."

"Reception bad down there?"

"Extremely."

A weird feeling blooms on the back of my neck as I walk out of the store. Sitcom Dad is nowhere to be found when I glance back.

"Can you repeat the last thirty seconds, please?" I ask. "I totally missed it."

"I was just saying that the neighbor unlocked the gate onto the property for you. The road past the gate is a mess. I hate to ask you this, but I need at least one picture of the clearing at the end."

"Good thing I brought my hiking boots."

"You're prepared. I like it."

I slide into the driver's seat. Ripley shoves her head under the phone so she can nibble my earlobe and let me know she's thrilled I'm back after leaving her alone in the car for approximately an eternity (five minutes). I push her away and buckle my seat belt.

"I've been accused of being overprepared at times."

We pull out of the gas station parking lot, the phone on my thigh and speaker on. I look in my rearview mirror to find Sitcom Dad standing where I was just parked, glaring after my truck.

"Better over than under. Listen." Ellis pauses like he's gathering his words. "Usually, I do these myself. It's the only way I get out on the road anymore, so I don't mind the more . . . uncomfortable aspects."

"I like driving, and I like hiking. This is perfect for me, honest."

"I appreciate that about you. Still, I don't feel great about sending someone alone. A sprained ankle in Columbus is a bad day; a sprained ankle alone out in the woods is a potential emergency."

"I understand." Emma and my mom worrying about me is a wound being agitated again and again. This though? This is new, and it feels good. "I'll be careful."

"Stick to the road, okay? Don't go wandering into the woods."

"Don't wander into the deep, dark woods. Got it. I'll make sure to keep my distance from houses on chicken legs."

He's quiet. The nice, good feeling of just a minute ago wilts.

"I'll stick to the road. Sorry."

"That's good. Thank you. I'm not trying to make you feel bad. To me, your safety isn't anything to joke about." His voice is warm and the humiliation of striking out on a joke fades a bit. "I'm going to be in meetings all day, but I'll have my phone with me. If you need anything, just call. At minimum, I want you to check in with me when you're done, okay? It'd really help my peace of mind."

"Okay. I will."

"Great. I'll let you get to it. I'll talk to you later, Lou."

The call ends on the tail end of my "Bye."

I roll my eyes at men and their poor phone skills, but

mostly I'm trying not to smile. I got to be mean to a man, I'm getting paid to go on a long walk with my dog, *and* Ellis is worrying about me.

This is shaping up to be a damn good day.

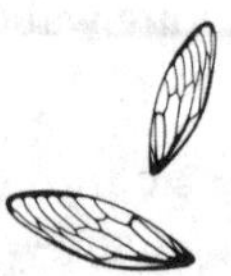

Terri: The case we're covering today is in southern Ohio. We're talking hills. We're talking cornfields and lots and lots of trees. Rolling Appalachian Mountains with small towns thrown in for flavor.

Naomi: Midwest Gothic. No, wait! Monsanto Gothic.

Terri [laughs]: I'll be honest, this was a hard case to research. What I did find is pretty wild, so bear with me. Okay, Jamie Tennyson was thirty-four years old when he went missing. He was quiet and kind, he worked in IT, and he was an amateur photographer. Remember the photography bit, it comes up later. So, on June 25, 2001, Jamie drove two hours south from Ohio's capital, Columbus, to Lawrence County. It's super rural, tons of hiking trails and camping. I sent you some pictures.

Naomi: It's pretty. Lots of caves. You know how I feel about caves.

Terri: Not every disappearance can be blamed on heretofore unearthed cave systems.

Naomi: But can this one?

Terri [sighs]: I'll let you tell me.

~~~~~~~~~~

Lovely Dark & Deep: Missing in the Woods Podcast
~~~~~~~~~~

CHAPTER 3

I take the country curves slow despite the rising urge to press on the pedal until I can feel the speed in my chest.

There's nothing like rushing down a rural road on a summer day with cicadas singing in the trees above you. The whole world is humming. It's invigorating. Especially after a week spent in the city in an office with people who won't stop talking about personal development and the powers of herbal tea. Wind whips through the car. It strips the cloying frustration that's built up in my body. I feel lighter, cleaner, less weighed down than I have in days. Weeks, actually.

Has it really been weeks since I felt this good?

For a brief, intense moment, I'm overcome with the memory of driving through Hocking Hills with my mom. She loved living in the country. She loved the fog that drifted through the trailers in the morning and the deer that wandered through the homes at dusk. Don't get either of those in the trailer park we moved to the summer before college so I wouldn't have to pay for campus housing.

Affording tuition even with scholarships and student loans and a million summer jobs was a struggle. Would it have been possible? I'd have to work nonstop, but yeah. My mom insisted that in the end it'd be worth it.

She was right. Her moving out of the country and to Columbus so I could live at home and commute to classes saved me literal thousands. I had to be grateful. I *was* grateful. That didn't stop the gratefulness existing hand in hand with guilt that she sacrificed another thing for my sake.

Her love of being outside is the reason I started drawing in the first place. She'd take me to a park—not with swings and slides and Astroturf, but one where the woods were thick, and the creeks ran quick and clear.

Most of the time my eyes were down to look for cool rocks or weird sticks or feathers plucked from a bird's wing and hidden in the underbrush. By the end my pockets were full and my stomach was squirming in anticipation of giving them to her when we got home.

I was always trying to give my mother something. A report card with all A's; a rock with a hole through the middle; a clean house for her to come home to after a long shift; a meal she didn't have to cook; a safe place to talk about the things that hurt her, about the things she never told anyone else.

Eventually, the things I tried to give her after our walks were too much.

"How 'bout you just pick one and draw it when we get home," she said. The forest debris from that day was laid out on our peeling laminate table. Her hair was slicked back in a tight ponytail that she hadn't taken down since she got home from work. "One special thing I can keep. Okay?"

I kept it up, and she kept them all. I had the drawings bound into a book for Mother's Day the year I graduated high school. Having the finished product in my hands inspired the children's book I've been trying to illustrate since my first-semester art class.

One Special Thing, a mother and daughter's relationship as told through drawings of the objects found on their walks through the woods.

There'd be no more walks in the woods until she was feeling better. Maybe not even then. She's almost sixty now. Being an STNA had wrecked her body at a pace that none of my cubicle coworkers would ever experience.

I don't really want to think about that, so I don't.

The hills open up into a valley pockmarked with one-story ranches. The homes disappear entirely after the directions prompt me to turn onto Harmon Road. It's a one-lane dirt-and-scattered-gravel excuse for a thoroughfare. Leaves from last year's fall litter the stormwater ditches along either side. The air smells dark and earthy—the good kind of decomposition. No maggots squirming in eye sockets, no flesh melting off brittle bones, just leaves falling to bits and wood turning dark and tender.

It's fifteen minutes on Harmon Road before a house appears. It's tucked into the low point of forested hills. A roof that's more moss than shingle, and a sagging wood porch that's been bleached by the sun peek through the trees.

The road goes up a hill tall enough I can't see who might

be coming up the other side. I slow and move over as much as I can without sliding into the ditch to my right. Cresting the hill reveals another hill beyond.

A half mile later, there's another home. This one is newer. Robin's-egg blue siding, a gleaming dark gray metal roof, a brand-new Jeep in the driveway without a single spot of dirt on it.

We go another mile up soft, nameless hills, bumping through mud puddles, with not a single house in sight. Finally, the road curves to reveal a brilliantly red gate stretching the width of the road.

I park six or so yards away and turn to Ripley. "Ready for a walk?"

She perks up at the *W* word and presses her nose to the passenger-side window, leaving a cloudy smear. Bringing my dog for an inspection is not allowed. We're in the middle of nowhere though. Who's gonna know?

The air is thick with the scent of growing things and sun-warmed earth. For the first time in weeks, I'm not just some shape floating through space, but actually connected to the world.

Ripley is practically vibrating when I open the passenger-side door. My water bottle goes into my backpack, I drape her slip lead across my shoulders, and a note with my information and reason for being here goes on the dashboard.

"Break." I give her release word. Ripley leaps out, does a big stretch, and sets off sniffing the edges of the forest.

She wouldn't be allowed off leash in a more populated setting. Not because of her, but because of untrained people and their untrained dogs. I've spent hours upon hours socializing and training Ripley. Any extra money or time I managed to scrape together went to trying new things with her: dock diving, lure chasing, scent work. But who has the time, let alone the money, to pursue any of those things consistently? Not me.

All that work means I now have a well-balanced, responsive dog that's indifferent to other animals, fully ignores new humans, and can be trusted to snuffle around in the woods.

The truck beeps when I lock it once, twice, three times, because what if the first two didn't work? You never know. Gotta make sure.

"Ripley, here," I say when I get to the gate.

She abandons snorting around a clump of grass and runs to me. In a rush of white teeth and a pink mouth, she takes a treat from my hand.

The gate is composed of thick metal painted red. A shiny chain wrapped in snaking loops around the middle keeps it closed. Cicadas' exoskeletons dangle from the red metal. Thickets have grown over the barbed wire fence at each end of the gate.

I'm about to tug on the chain to see if it's open like Ellis said when I see it.

See them.

There's something on the gate, mostly obscured by overgrowth, and I have to move a bit of the brush aside to see clearly.

There are . . . things . . . hanging from the rusted bars. Things woven from dried grass and thin sticks, threatening and jagged.

Three circles, each with two sticks intersecting in the center. It's the Zodiac Killer symbol, or what the Zodiac symbol was meant to be: crosshairs. Two small, hollow pieces of wood hang from each of the crosshairs. They're attached by thin twine and make a soft *tock*, *tock*, *tock* sound when they knock together.

This doesn't feel like someone's weird little arts and crafts project. It feels like a threat.

I should get in the truck and drive away. Every true crime podcast ever and Emma's voice tell me that I really, *really* should.

I take out my phone to call her. No bars. The phone itself is hot, which means that in about a week it'll randomly turn off and never turn on again.

I stare at the gate, and it stares back.

Emma would say this job isn't important enough to risk getting serial-killed or assaulted by a weirdo in the woods.

Except . . . isn't it though? This job was supposed to save us. This job was supposed to be the rope I used to climb my way out of generational poverty and bring my mom with me. Ellis is giving me a second chance, one that I will not get again if I choose not to walk through this gate.

I dig the small hatchet out of my backpack. It's so sharp that it's hard to focus my eyes on the edge. I give it an experimental twirl, then stick it in an outer loop on my backpack.

If anything weird happens, we can turn back.

"Okay," I say, and Ripley looks up at me, no less excited this time. "Let's go."

CHAPTER 4

No howling ghosts or slinking demons emerge from the forest when we walk through the gate. No haunting instrumentals erupt to herald my trip into a cursed dimension. No whispers of leaves crunching under the feet of a murderer.

I do hear Emma berating me.

What is wrong with you, Lou? Do you want to die?

My internal Emma shuts up when I answer, *Yeah, sometimes I do.* Sometimes the urge to no longer exist feels like the only thing that belongs to me.

The trees are tall and thick-leaved. Since a lot of the sunlight is blocked by the canopy there isn't much vegetation on the forest floor other than ferns, leggy bushes, and other shade-tolerant plants. A lot of raspberry thorns and honey locust spikes. Sharp things growing in dim light.

The path itself is pockmarked with dark puddles of standing water, full of last year's leaves and floating cicada corpses.

Ripley's initial overwhelming excitement of being in a

new place with new smells fades after ten minutes of walking. Instead of jumping from one patch of grass to the other, she snuffs slowly through leaves and fallen branches, glancing back at me to make sure I'm still there.

"Ack!" I say when she tries to lap at one of the puddles. She looks back at me as if to ask why I'm being so cruel. "It's gross, that's why."

Talking to my dog is one of the things Jena and Arden didn't seem to understand when I used to tell them stories about my life. What else am I supposed to talk about when we're sitting around the lunch table? Children? I have none. Dating? Hard pass. The deterioration of the nation and the growing wealth gap? Hell no.

Jena finds a way to link whatever I say to Ascent. As far as I can tell, Ascent is 30 percent bootstraps and pulling yourself up by them; 30 percent the soul-deep fear of never making back the cost you've sunk into classes and retreats and seminars; and 40 percent telling people the reason the world has not been saved is because you (*specifically* you) have not yet devoted yourself to becoming as rich as humanly possible and donating your excess wealth to charities doing maximally efficient work—also known as effective altruism; and until you (*specifically* you) decide to commit every second of every day to hustling, the world and everyone in it will continue to suffer and die.

It is just so extremely convenient and purely a coincidence that the quickest way to amass wealth is by becoming your own small business owner by selling Ascent classes to the people who need it most: your friends and family!

The Ascent Discovery Weekend left me feeling jangled and raw. Three days, Friday to Sunday, 8 AM to 8 PM. Workshop after class after breakout session—all about you, your faults, the power of your own brain. They crack you open just to empty you out, and then fill you up again.

"It's going to peel back all that armor, babe," Jena told me on the very first morning. "But we'll both be here for you."

And they were.

Either Jena or Arden met me in the conference hall for breakfast with a latte or Americano each morning. They sat with me while I sipped my drink and ate a bagel, and they asked questions about how I was feeling, what I thought about the workshops. All three of us met for lunch. Every day. Their focus was entirely on me. It felt like being held.

And then it was over. I got home, took a shower, and the magic of the hot water on my skin brought me right back down to earth.

"It's a thousand bucks," my mom had said the day before the weekend.

She was sitting at her usual spot at the kitchen table. A thin line of smoke drifted from the end of her cigarette. It was quickly swept out the window by a cool spring breeze.

"You know what we could do with a thousand bucks? Used to be you could get a Tony Robbins book for fifteen dollars in the eighties. Same junk in that book as this three-day bullshit."

"I know," I said, stirring sugar into my coffee a little more aggressively than strictly necessary. "It's just what you're supposed to do. Like, networking or something. It's all part of my corporate-ladder-climbing plan."

"I don't understand any of that. You shouldn't do things you don't like just 'cause you think you need to take care of me. I can take care of myself. I've been doing it my whole life."

She flicked her cigarette on the edge of her ashtray too hard. She was angry—the sort of angry that could only be defined by the few things at which it *wasn't* aimed. That was almost exclusively me and Ripley.

We'd had this conversation before. Just like all those other times, I didn't know what to say. After all she'd told me—about being kicked out of the house at sixteen by her alcoholic parents, about dropping out of high school, how much it hurt that sometimes patients told her she was stupid for being *just* an STNA—I didn't understand how she could expect I'd want to do anything else other than take care of her.

I leaned down to hug her one-armed. She leaned into it, then away.

So, yeah, I agreed the whole personal development, self-help thing was woo-woo bullshit. But if it put me in their good graces? I'd grit my teeth and do it.

I focus on walking and throwing an increasingly slobbery stick for Ripley instead of work thoughts.

The concept of these hills being older than bones makes sense when you're walking through them. Trees in this area are tall. Some are so thick a person could wrap their arms around them and their fingertips wouldn't touch.

It's less the growth that gives the feeling of age. It's more the smell. Age in these hills smells like ozone and earth; it smells like pulped green matter and trickling streams hidden under fallen leaves; it feels like the vibrating pulse of thousands of cicadas in the trees.

At the end of the road sits the charred skeleton of a house. Grass as tall as a person and other flowering plants have reclaimed the space. There's a sweet smell in the air, mixed with the metal tang of nutrient-rich soil. It's all kind of beautiful actually—the blackened bones of a former home rising out of new growth.

A big oak tree, felled by some storm, lies to the left. I climb up onto it to get a better vantage for the pictures. I line up the shot, shoot from a few angles, and wish I had something to draw the scene with.

Ripley tears through the grass in erratic shapes, doing her best impersonation of a jumping gazelle. I watch her, feeling light and airy and *happy* because I get to inhabit such a beautiful place with my ridiculous dog.

That's when I see the small mound of hair and skin that used to be an animal.

The air is so pregnant with the constant drone of cicadas that the buzz of flies didn't even register. Up on this log, the crushed circle of grass and the corpse sprawled through the center is perfectly visible.

The raccoon's chest is split open. White rib bones and yellow fat dot the red expanse of fresh, glistening blood. Strips of skin and tufts of hair litter the ground. Its front leg lies a few feet away. The flesh is ragged where the limb was ripped from its body.

Beyond the raccoon is another patch of crushed grass. What lies within is darker and smaller but similarly mangled. A third circle of flattened grass sits halfway between the log and the house. It's far enough away to be mostly obscured by the wildflowers and grass.

Whatever's in it is larger than the two decimated bodies.

A gust of wind moves through the meadow. The grass around the larger body sways and separates enough to offer a two-second glimpse inside.

A coyote, its head low and snout dark, stares through the vegetation. It's big. Taller than Ripley. Its legs are thin, but long. They terminate at an emaciated body covered in a coat of mangy, tufted hair.

The air goes still. The coyote becomes a dark shape obscured by the grass once more.

Ripley is no longer running. Her nose is in the air, twitching. She shifts so she's facing the direction of the coyote.

"Ripley," I say, hushed. Her ear twitches, but she doesn't budge. "Ripley, *come.*"

One beat, another, her nose keeps twitching. A third beat, and finally she walks to me.

Relief is a visceral rush. I've never been so glad to have spent hours upon hours on her training. The good feeling is immediately doused by the coyote's growl. It's low and unsteady. Almost warbling.

I step off the fallen oak and immediately regret losing

sight of the coyote's shadow in the grass. It's a false sense of safety, being able to see the danger.

My mom got me a can of pepper spray when I started going on hikes with Ripley. I put it in the side pocket of my backpack and never touched it again. Now, I uncap it and hold it at the ready. The hatchet is an option, but only as a last resort. I'm the one that interrupted its lunch. The coyote is just being a coyote. Plus, it'd need to be too damn close for it to be effective.

I back up toward the path. Not running, but not slowly either. Ripley sticks close. Though her fur is up and she keeps looking over her shoulder.

We're almost at the path when the coyote steps from the meadow. I freeze at the sight of it. Probably a bad idea. Probably I should keep moving, but I don't. Instead, I stop and stare.

Lines of drool drip from its mouth. Something, mud or maybe dried blood, coats the animal's legs and stomach. Whatever it is, it's dark. Almost black.

The coyote takes a few quick steps forward, then stops. It opens its mouth wide, wider, wider still like it's trying to crack its jaw but can't. It bites at the air and that too seems unsatisfying, because it does it again.

This is not a coyote guarding its meal. This animal is sick.

Not just sick. *Rabid.*

It wavers sideways, then abruptly sits, revealing its profile. The coyote's back leg has been entirely degloved. Raw, red flesh stretches from the animal's paw to midway up its thigh.

What could have done something like that? A sympathetic shiver catches in my chest. How must that have *felt*? The sensation of skin rending from the meat underneath. I hope its brain was already thoroughly cooked when it happened.

I let out a shaky breath and keep backing up. It continues to flex its jaw and stare into the middle distance, seemingly unaware of our presence.

In a few yards we'll be out of sight down a slight curve in the road. Maybe this'll end up being nothing more than a good story to tell at real estate conferences. Katsaros will joke about my employer-provided insurance being top-notch if I do need a rabies shot. Everyone will laugh and laugh.

Of course, this is when the coyote chooses to stand. It wavers. For a second it looks like it's about to sit again.

Instead, it swings its head to look at us.

And then it starts running.

Terri: He arrived at the cabin his company was renting for a leadership retreat on Friday around 3 PM. There's not much information about what happened between him getting there and when he disappeared. I tried to find someone from his job. Either they changed their name or it doesn't exist anymore. I even did a public records request, but it was denied.

Naomi: Did they give a reason why?

Terri: It's still active, so they can't give the case file out.

Naomi: It's been, like, sixteen years. Literally the definition of cold.

Terri: Tell that to the Lawrence County Sheriff Department. But actually don't, because they're *so* rude. So, Jamie and four of his coworkers decide to go on a hike before they went home. They get going around noon. Jamie's at the back of the group. He's lingering, taking pictures of the scenery, enjoying himself. It's all normal, until about forty-five minutes into the hike when the person in front of Jamie turns around . . . and he's gone.

Naomi: No! I hate these ones. They freak me out so bad.

Terri: It's because someone literally disappearing in the woods is legit terrifying. So, the group called for Jamie, no answer. They backtracked down the trail, didn't find anything. After two hours, they called the cops. There was a search, but I couldn't find any info on how long it lasted or how it was conducted. And . . . That's pretty much it. The last article about it was published in early 2002. After that, nothing.

Naomi: Terri. You can't do this to me. That's it? They didn't find anything?

Terri: I didn't say that.

Lovely Dark & Deep: Missing in the Woods Podcast

CHAPTER 5

We run.

The coyote is so much faster even though it's stumbling every few feet. In just a few seconds it'll have caught up to our meager head start. The pepper spray won't reach. I've got no way of knowing if it even has enough brain left to respond to stimulus. Instead, I stuff the spray in the side pocket of my backpack, grab the nearest fist-sized rock, and hurl it as hard as I can.

The rock strikes just above the coyote's eye. It stops, head low and gaze unfocused.

There's something wrong with its ear. The cartilage dangles like it's been snapped. But no . . . that's not right. Because its two ears are still right where they belong on the top of its head. Is it skin? Did a piece of its face slump away from its skull when the rock hit? Is that what happened to its back leg? Does rabies make skin wilt from a body like damp wallpaper?

I don't wait to figure it out.

Mud squelches around my hiking boots with every pounding step up the road. Sweat stings my eyes and chafes the skin under my backpack straps.

We've been running for a few minutes. If the coyote's following, then it's doing so out of view. My ribs cramp from the combination of cardio and sucking down big lungfuls of humid air. I slow to a fast walk and hope I don't end up with rabies because my cardio is shit.

My heart jolts at the sight of the red gate.

The runes clink against the metal bars when I push through. A surge of tense, sweaty relief washes over me at the sight of the truck.

I bend mid-stride, slip my arm under Ripley's chest, and pick her up in one motion. She jerks, surprised, but doesn't struggle. Ripley weighs forty-seven pounds, but she might as well be light as air. She squirms out of my grip into the passenger seat as soon as we're in the truck. The sound of the locks clicking is pure relief.

"Fuck this," I tell Ripley, and stick the key in the ignition.

I turn it.

Nothing happens.

I turn the key again.

Nothing.

The battery can't be dead, can it? Did I leave the lights on? A cursory glance around the truck confirms that no, they're all off. There's gas in the tank. It got serviced two months back and nothing came up. There's no reason for this to be happening.

I try the key again. Just in case.

Nope. Nothing.

"Okay. Okay, it's fine. This is fine." Ripley is watching me. She's panting because we're in a closed car on a summer day. "I'm fine. You're okay." I go to pet her. She ducks away when I move too quickly.

I suck in a breath. I am *not* going to cry because I'm freaking out, which in turn is freaking my dog out. I'm really, really *not* going to do that.

Just try to calm down. Focus on what you can see, smell, or hear. My toes are wet, and I can smell the mud on my shoes and Ripley's paws. My backpack is pressing into my lower back. The hatchet rests across my thighs. Sweat drips in rivulets down my neck and back.

I shoulder my backpack off, plop Ripley's expandable bowl in the cup holder, and pour out an inch of water from my bottle. She laps it up sloppily. I take a swig and nearly choke when my other hand brushes the mesh pocket holding my phone. I have a phone. I can call someone to come get me out of this mess. I've never felt so stupid and so relieved at once.

"I'm just gonna call Emma," I tell Ripley.

Emma will know what to do. She'll approve of calling her from inside the car instead of leaving myself vulnerable to a rabid animal attack outside. She'll understand the situation and will have a practical solution that'll fix all of it.

The call screen is up, but it's not connecting. I end the call and try again. Same thing—call screen, no dialing. The data is on and there's a whole bar. It's the middle of the month, so it's not the phone bill being late.

I try her again, then AAA, then 911. I text her, but it won't switch from "sending" to "sent," and I think taking a tally of the sensations in my body won't help the panic attack coming on this time. I turn the phone off and on and try it all again.

I try my mom. That one rings, but there's no answer at the end. It doesn't ring the second time I dial her number. I'm not surprised she didn't answer though.

She had to work twelve-hour shifts all the time when I was a kid. She didn't have anyone to watch me and didn't have money for a babysitter. We came up with a code: One call means it's not urgent; twice means call back as soon as you can; three times means the house is actively burning down and she needs to answer right now or else.

If the second call went through, she'd answer. But it didn't go through, so she didn't.

By the time I've cycled through calling and texting for help, it's getting hard to breathe from how stifling the heat is inside the truck.

I stare out the front window at the gate. It's still there, too far away to see the symbols. Runes? A weird art project? The woods continue to be woods around me.

"Maybe it's gone."

It didn't seem to follow us after I whanged it with the rock. The poor thing was in bad shape. It very well could have keeled over and died as soon as I turned my back. There's a strong possibility the danger is over.

Regardless, we have to get out of the truck.

It's incredible how much cooler the air is outside. Ripley hops out and immediately shakes herself. I wipe my face with my shirt and take another swallow of water. The cool descent down my throat into my stomach is a sin.

I take a minute to breathe and scan the area around us. There's a smell I didn't notice in my panic. It's chemical and sickeningly strong. I recognize it immediately.

There are puddles everywhere. One has a weird glint to it.

Water leaches into the knees of my jeans when I kneel in the mud. I point my phone's flashlight under the truck and immediately wish I hadn't.

A lake of liquid shining with rainbow bright chemicals. Gas. Gas mixed with mud; gas mixed with rainwater; gas that would get us home drained out of the tank and onto the ground.

There is a hole the size of my index finger in the gas tank above. The hole is neat. Smooth. Circular. I press my finger to it.

A curled plastic shaving sticks to my skin. I sit back on my haunches so I can hold the finger and the piece up to eye level. Ripley goes to lick my hand, then raises a lip and shakes her head at the smell of gas.

I have the strongest urge to keep the tiny piece of plastic. There's no reason for it. I just want it. I wonder if the person who drilled a hole in my gas tank wants to keep me too.

CHAPTER 6

On the left is the new-construction home I passed on my way in.

It's encased in robin's-egg blue siding and bordered by precise boxwood landscaping planted in beds of fragrant mulch. The dark metal roof brings the whole look together. Track marks from large construction vehicles mark the ground at the edges of the woods and along the driveway. A sporty little Audi sits in the driveway. It has the energy of a frat bro brushing behind me at a dorm party and "accidentally" tugging my ass back into its groin. Wasn't there a Jeep before?

I am drenched in sweat and sucking in air through my nose to try to calm my thudding heart. We alternated between jogging and fast walking the mile from my useless hunk of a truck to the intersecting road.

Ripley is panting—saliva slicking her snout and dripping from her tongue. Running in this heat is not good for her. She keeps looking at me like she doesn't understand why I'm making her do it.

I don't know how to break it to a dog that (1) you think someone has deliberately stranded both her and her person in the middle of the woods, (2) that her owner's phone won't connect to anyone despite having service, (3) that both of them somehow have to get to a phone that does work in order to get help, and, finally, (4) do so while avoiding being serial-killed, or axe-murdered, or attacked by a rabid coyote.

There's a house farther down the road. I know this because I specifically made a mental note to put both it and the new-construction home into my report. The other house was set too far back to see much of the actual building from the road. What was visible were sun-bleached deer figurines, ragged windmills that had long ago lost their shine, and a crooked mailbox.

One of the curtains in the new-construction house twitches. It's a second-story bow window that juts out of the house. Panes of glass like many boxy eyes glint down at me with over-Windexed intensity. That's how I'd draw it—each window an eye and the front door a grotesque mouth. The curtain doesn't move again. There's a rock lying a few inches from my right foot that would shatter the bright-eyed windows spectacularly.

I keep walking.

I'm not sure how I'm going to explain this objectively silly decision to Emma or my mother. How do you explain to someone that, yes, you were in fear for your life, but the Audi reminded you of the coked-out, dull-as-sea-glass frat boys you went to school with and the distant, unsympathetic length of their gazes?

How do you explain that you were desperate for a phone to call for help, but that you used to deliver pizzas to houses that looked just like this, and they always contained pinch-lipped women and bunched-up men who took the time to write in a zero for the tip?

How do you explain, without sounding utterly ridiculous, that you don't trust people with money to the extent that it means walking another half mile through the woods to find help?

"Let's go," I tell Ripley. She doesn't move. She's facing the way we came.

She's going to hear someone following us long before I do.

I stare hard in the same direction, waiting for either a blood-splattered, axe-wielding killer or a mangy coyote to come trotting around the curve in the road. Statistically, it's more likely to be a common-looking white man in a button-down with an office job than a serial killer.

A bell goes *ding ding ding* in my head. Speaking of common white men. I did piss off one at the gas station.

I would have noticed if I was being followed though, right? If a car was tailing me from the gas station to the inspection site, I would have seen it. It would have been noticeable out here in the country.

Unless there's some other trail or path or road I don't know about.

No, no, stop it. Don't make shit up. Be calm. Focus on what you can see or smell or hear.

Ripley's focus breaks. Whatever held her attention is gone. Or gone quiet.

We keep moving—this time in a fast walk. Half a mile later we're standing in front of deer figurines and motionless windmills. The mailbox has a faded sunflower painted on the side.

"Killers don't paint sunflowers. Do they?"

Ripley looks at me to see if I'm gonna tell her to do something, then snuffs at the weeds around the mailbox's post when I don't.

"Sure hope not."

It's not a long driveway. The front porch isn't nearly as decrepit as it seemed from the road. It's mostly just old and sun-bleached. There's a shed at the side of the house that's just as sun-bleached. I knock before I can think twice. There's movement inside—heavy steps and the creak of old wood under the weight of a moving body.

A man opens the door. He's old, is my first thought. My second is that despite him being elderly, I do not think I could fight him off. He's at least six feet and bulky in a way that working people get when they have a steady diet of manual labor and cheap, carb-heavy food.

He stares at me, not saying anything.

"Hi!" I say in a chipmunk voice that makes me wince. "Hi. My truck is out of gas and my phone isn't working and I just, if I could use your phone? Or I could wait here while you use it to call . . . someone. I'm not from this area but I'm pretty sure triple-A won't come out here, you know?"

He clears his throat in a way that suggests it being chronic. His gaze finds Ripley. Whatever he sees makes him frown deeper than he was before.

"She's friendly. She won't be any trouble—"

"Your dog's hot."

"Yeah. We were moving pretty fast." She's also entirely black and a bully breed. Neither of which are particularly good for respiration.

He stares, then turns away. Just before he shuts the door he says, "Put her in the backyard."

Maybe we're about to be murdered, but she needs water and I need a phone. Behind the ranch-style home is a quaint yard. Sunflowers and tulips are painted in vibrant brushstrokes across the short white picket fence along the perimeter.

The gate opens smoothly. Everything in this yard is well taken care of. Doted on, even.

The sliding door opens. The cool breath of the AC chills the skin of my back where my shirt has ridden up. The man clears his throat. Definitely chronic.

"You can stay out there if you want, or you can come in. I'm not gonna mess with you either way. Your choice."

"If I come in, can I hold my hatchet?"

"Sure."

"Can I bring my dog?"

He looks at her with pinched lips. "Wipe her down first. Just cleaned the floors."

He disappears from the doorway and reappears with two damp floral hand towels that have seen better days. "No 'ffense, but you too."

It doesn't take long to wipe Ripley down and then brush the mud off my pants. I hesitate, but ultimately decide to kick the dirt off my shoes instead of taking them off. It's rude and kinda gross, but I'm more invested in being able to run away than I am in being polite.

The house smells like the mornings after my mom invited her coworkers over for a drink and a smoke. I'd wake up bleary-eyed after staying up late to listen to them laughing and talking. The whole house would smell of cigarettes and perfume and beer.

Her friends love her. They call her whenever they have a problem and no solution. No matter how exhausted she is, she has no-nonsense advice and stern yet compassionate words that draw people to her like a moth to a light. I used to sit on the stairs and listen while she told stories that were technically true, but also very embellished.

"The story's not the point," she told me one morning at the kitchen table. I'd just shown her sketches for *One Special Thing*. "It's how it makes people feel."

This is a good kitchen. There's enough space for two people to move comfortably around each other. A tiny circular table is tucked next to the sliding glass door. Cabinets the color of the sky just before a rain draws the eye toward the massive farmhouse sink set under a big, bright window. If I ever have enough money to buy a house for my mom, that is *exactly* the sink I'd put in her kitchen.

"I love your sink," I say when the old man returns with a cordless phone in his hand.

He sends a critical eye to the sink and huffs. "My wife did too. She was more excited 'bout that damn sink than any gift I ever got her. Think she might have been more excited 'bout that sink than our kid getting into Brown."

He hands over the cordless phone, and I thank him. I put the hatchet down on the table, careful not to scratch the surface, then sit. His back is to me as he fiddles around on the other side of the kitchen. Ripley stays standing next to me, her side pressed to my leg, her tail loose, and her eyes on the man. She's like me: initially suspicious, but generally friendly once she's had a chance to warm up to new company.

My phone's screen is dark when I fish it out of my pocket. It can't be dead, can it? The battery was full the last time I looked at it. It flashes when I restart it, then goes black again. Two more tries give the same results.

"Everything alright?" He sets a glass of ice water on the table, and a bowl on the floor for Ripley, then backs away to lean against the counter.

There's a water stain on his ceiling. I squint at it, then squint at the phone in my hand. This is starting to feel like a bad horror movie.

"My phone isn't working. The only number I have memorized is my mom's, but she's sick and . . . I can't call her." Knuckling my eyes doesn't take away the gritty feeling. I've been meaning to memorize Emma's for the last few years. I just . . . haven't.

"What's your name?" he asks.

"Lou."

"'M Clarence." He pulls out the seat opposite and sits. "I could look up triple-A's number. Like you said, I doubt they come all the way out here. Might be better off with the local mechanic in that case. I got his number in my Rolodex."

"Not sure a mechanic can fix my problem . . ." I trail off, extremely aware of coming off hysterical or paranoid, and settle on just facts. "I think maybe, I mean I'm not sure, but . . . I think someone drilled a hole in my gas tank."

Clarence clicks his tongue. "Well, no. A mechanic wouldn't be able to help you with that problem. The sheriff, now. That might be an option."

The idea of talking to a cop with Ripley by my side makes my skin crawl.

Growing up in trailer parks inhabited by people who are very, very poor and almost always marginalized in one way or several has instilled within me a healthy fear of, and deep anger at, the police. Being in a crisis where I am afraid and Ripley is stressed and there's a cop in front of us who's probably in fear for his life for no good reason at all seems like a terrible idea.

I nod anyway. It's the only option that might not result in Emma yelling at me. And honestly, what else am I supposed to do? This is what they're supposed to be *for*, right? Maybe having Clarence with us will be enough of a shield to keep the situation from escalating.

Clarence gets up to retrieve a much-creased copy of the local yellow pages. He flips to the page with the sheriff's number and turns it to face me. "You want to dial them? No speaker on this phone."

I smile. I can't help it. Clarence raises his bushy eyebrows in question.

"Felt pretty stupid not knocking on that house down the road. I'm glad I didn't."

He makes a face like he sucked a lemon. "I got no idea who woulda opened it. It's a rental. People comin' and goin' all the goddamn time."

I tell him he can dial, then listen as he speaks to someone about getting Sheriff Cory on the line, then to him breathing while he waits. Ripley finally relaxes enough to flop down on her side. She jerks her legs at me until I scratch at the soft skin of her belly.

Clarence hangs up and frowns out the sliding glass doors. "He'll be down in thirty, an hour tops."

"An *hour*?"

"That's what he said. Never met a man of the law that I liked, but this one is something special. Even his daddy was better, and he had a mind like a bucket of rocks." He fixes me a look, his eyebrows drawn down. "You want me to drive you up there so you don't have to wait?"

"Maybe?" I knuckle my eyes. "I didn't really want to talk to the cops in the first place. Do you have Wi-Fi? I could use your computer to message my friend?"

He shakes his head and pulls an actual flip phone out of his pocket. "No Internet out here. If I need it, I go to the library. They got computers you can use. I could take you there."

I hesitate. I don't know which is the right choice.

Clarence regards me. "How 'bout this. You lemme see if I got a charger for that phone. If I do, you plug it in, get your friend's number, and then you make a decision. If I don't got a charger or your phone don't work, I drive you up to the library."

"Yeah. Yeah, okay. That sounds good."

Clarence rises from the table like a creaky doll unwinding its parts. When he comes back, he has three different charging cables and a USB port in his hands.

"My daughter can't keep a cord to save her life. She leaves and an hour later I get a call, 'Daddy, is my charger there?'" He shakes his head, a fond smile on his mouth.

Once plugged in, my phone gives a buzz. The light in the corner blinks, but the screen remains black. There's nowhere for the helpless frustration in my chest to go. I knew it was going to crap out eventually, but right *now*? It's too awful of a coincidence to be real.

The sliding glass doors are very clean and provide a perfect view of the yard and the trees beyond. A thin sapling sways while everything else around it remains still.

"What?" Clarence asks.

"That house at the end of the road. The one that's burnt? My boss sent me down there to get pictures of it for an appraisal. There was a coyote down there. It chased us. I'm pretty sure it's rabid. I haven't seen it since, but I don't know. I keep feeling like it's gonna pop out of the woods like Cujo or something."

He motions his chin toward the trees. "Couple days ago, I was walking the creek. Cuts through the McLaren property down the road. Got rushed by a skunk. Sucker didn't even try to spray me. Just wanted to bite. Lucky, I had this." He reaches for an umbrella stand full of walking sticks.

He pulls one out that's chunky and hand-carved. "Took the body to the county sheriff's office. Told them it needed testing. They swore they'd get down there to check it out."

He peers outside. The sapling that was swaying is now still. *Everything* is still in the stagnant, windless heat.

Wind chimes hung throughout the yard have been providing sweet trilling background music since the moment I arrived. Their silence only magnifies the feeling that something's gearing up to come charging out of the trees to shatter the quiet.

Clarence frowns at me. "I'm calling Cory again. Got a woman being terrorized in my house, and he can't hurry his ass up."

He goes to the living room with the phone held up to his ear. I stare out the door until Ripley pushes her head under my hand.

I flinch when my phone vibrates, then powers on. I tap in my password and try to bring up my recently called list.

There's a delay that makes me want to smash the screen on the kitchen counter. Finally, Emma's name pops up just below Ellis's. I tap on her name and . . . nothing. The screen has stopped registering any input. I try Ellis and that won't work either. I stare hard at the numbers below Emma's name. I run them through my brain three times before the phone goes black again.

"Good news and bad news," Clarence says when he returns to the kitchen. "Shelley down at the station radioed Cory and he's closer than she thought. Should be here in no time."

"What's the bad news?"

"Same as the good news. You get the honor of meeting the self-satisfied prick in person."

"That bad?"

"Thinks he's John Wayne. That working?" He gestures to my phone. He sucks his lip when I tell him no, it's not, but that I got Emma's number.

He's handing me the phone when there's a knock on the door.

Clarence looks down at his watch and shakes his head. "Fastest that man's moved in his entire life."

At first, I think the feeling that spears through my chest at the sound is panic, but it's not. It's doom. It's the sense that whatever's on the other side of that door is bad, bad, bad and that we should hide, hunker down, stay safe.

I say nothing, and watch as Clarence opens the door.

Sheriff Cory walks into Clarence's living room with his hand on his gun and a sunburn peeling the ridges of his cheeks. He's white, lean, and a little taller than my very average five feet seven inches. The sheriff's eyes are friendly in the way they usually are. Brown and helpful until they crack your skull or shoot your dog.

Cops are only friendly up until the sudden and painful moment they aren't.

"Place is looking good, Clarence." The sheriff nods and looks around until his eyes fall on me in the kitchen. "Whatcha got there?"

"A hatchet." I look at his hand on his gun. "What's *that*?"

He pauses. On the fifth beat, he raises both hands and

smiles wide. "Sorry! Habit. I used to work in the city. Dangerous place. Sometimes I forget to tone it down."

Behind him, Clarence looks to the ceiling like he's asking for patience. "Why dontcha sit, Cory. Lou's having some trouble. Let her tell you about it."

The sheriff sits on a floral couch so ancient I wonder if the house was built up around it. He says please when Clarence asks if he wants a glass of ice water.

"That dog under control?" The sheriff smiles in a way that can only be described as smarmy.

I look at Ripley, who is sitting quietly beside me, then up at the sheriff. Are *you*? I want to ask. I want to tell him to go fuck himself, but I can't. Ripley is my responsibility, and the most important thing is to get her out of these woods alive. Being polite is the straightest path to that destination.

"Yes. She's very well-trained."

He looks at the hatchet. "You gonna put that thing away?"

I don't want to, but I slip it into its loop on my backpack anyhow.

Clarence brings in the requested water, then sits. The sheriff motions to the floral armchair opposite him. I sit with my hand on Ripley's collar. She shifts, and I loosen my grip.

Silence draws out till it's thin as a razor.

Clarence clears his throat. "Why don't you start at the beginning, Lou."

"I work for a real estate appraisal company. My boss sent me here to photograph the McLaren parcel down the road.

When I got back to my truck it wouldn't start. Someone had drilled a hole in the gas tank."

The sheriff leans back and looks between Clarence and me. "Anything else?"

Clarence tells him about the rabid coyote. "You get that skunk I brought to the station a few days ago tested?"

The sheriff rubs a hand across his face. "It's the property owner's responsibility."

Clarence's every word is enunciated with prejudice. "William McLaren is an eighty-six-year-old retiree living in Florida with his son. You expect him to fly up here? It's a public health issue. You're s'pposed to be the sheriff last time I checked."

"Mr. McLaren sold earlier this year. I'm sure this is just some sort of misunderstanding. Frankly, I think you woulda been better off with a mechanic than me."

Shame and frustration heat my cheeks. I want to crush his nose with my fist. When he stands, Clarence and I follow.

"Look, roads out here are rough. It's easy to nick something when you're not used to it. Still, I don't want to dismiss your concerns and get myself canceled." He lifts a sardonic eyebrow.

Smarmy.

"Why don't you come up to the station with me, and we'll get a tow for your truck. Sound good?"

"Cory—"

The sheriff cuts Clarence off. "Sheriff."

Clarence's lips draw back. He enunciates his words

clearly. "Sheriff. If she says she thinks someone did it, I believe her. She's obviously scared."

"Not saying she's not scared. Just saying maybe it's not what she thinks. Either way, we'll get it resolved at the station."

He puts his arm out, motioning me to the front door ahead of him. I hesitate and look at Clarence.

"I'll follow," he says.

The sheriff doesn't argue, though he looks extremely annoyed. His car is an old black-and-white Crown Victoria with the air of a late-'90s buddy-cop movie. He opens the back door and motions for us to go inside.

"I can't sit in the front?"

"Nope. Rules are rules, even for a victim."

Victim. It bounces around inside my skull like an echo. What am I the victim of? A coyote that didn't even hurt me? My own paranoia?

Clarence puts his hand on my shoulder. I flinch in surprise. "S'alright. I'll be behind you the whole time."

I nod and slip out of my backpack. Get out of the woods. Get Ripley somewhere safe. Do both of those things as quickly as possible. I run Emma's number through my head again. I'll call her soon as I get to the station.

"Load up," I tell Ripley.

She hops in, and I follow. The car *smells* like a '90s buddy-cop movie: cheap cologne, sweat, and unwashed bodies. I clutch my backpack on my lap and rest my knuckles against the hatchet dangling from its loop. Ripley presses her nose against the window and pants in the heat of the car.

Sheriff Cory slides into the driver's seat and turns the key. He glances back at me through the metal grate.

"Hotter than a whore in hell." He shakes his head, then rolls down his window. "Almost forgot. Hey!"

Clarence, who was just about to climb into his ancient turquoise Ford truck, frowns at the sheriff waving him over. The sheriff shifts in his seat, doing something I can't see.

Clarence makes his slow, old-man way over. He stoops to look down through the window. "What's the problem—"

And then Clarence's head explodes.

Sometimes in a movie or a book or even a graphic novel, the world will freeze when something stunning and horrible happens. There's no freezing in this world. There's only red in the air like a mist, and Clarence's body crumpling on his front yard.

Ripley is barking and I'm yelling. I lunge for the door handle. Locked.

Sheriff Cory turns in his seat and aims a gun with a silencer at me. That's what I couldn't see. "You shut that mutt up or I'll shoot it."

I pull her close. "Ripley, enough."

Thankfully she listens. Still, her tail is tucked and she keeps making quiet little sounds of distress.

"Good," he says, and backs up out of the driveway.

I strain to see Clarence, to see if he's moving, if he's still alive, but I can't see him past the curve in the driveway.

"What are you doing? What's going on?"

Sheriff Cory glances at me in the rearview mirror, then looks back to the road. I slap the metal grate. My breath is coming too quick. My pulse is rushing in my ears. I think I'm having a panic attack.

What do I have on me? What can I *do*?

There's my hatchet. It's curved on one end and pointed at the other. I could break one of the windows with the pointed bit. It'd take at least three or four swings. The space is cramped. With Ripley taking up half of it I could easily hurt her. The sheriff could shoot her or me while I try to break it.

I glance down. The pepper spray is right where I put it after our encounter with the coyote.

Letting it off in an enclosed space is maybe the dumbest thing you could do with pepper spray. It literally says not to on the label. If we can't get out, both Ripley and I will be trapped in here with it. And him.

Something Emma said to me after recounting a story she heard on one of her favorite true crime podcasts comes to me.

"If you don't fight, you're fucked. If you do fight, you're still probably fucked.

"So you might as well just fight."

"He was kind," I say, slipping my hand into the side pocket. "And you're a piece of shit."

He cranks the radio, which is perfect because now he can't hear me uncapping the spray.

I raise it to the grate separating us. "Hey, asshole!"

He glances in the rearview mirror, then does a double take when he sees the spray. He half turns, his mouth open to say something.

Pepper spray hits him directly in the face.

He curses, and yells at me to "Fucking stop!" but I don't let up. I don't let up when my eyes, my lungs, my throat burn like I've swallowed hot coals. I don't let up when Ripley whimpers and wipes her paws over her eyes.

The car lurches to the side.

And then we're weightless.

An instinct in the back of my brain screams that weightlessness is *bad*, and I better hold on.

Before I can even brace myself, the car's front tires hit the ground. Pain explodes as the top of my head cracks on the ceiling. Ripley yelps when she falls from the seat into the footwell. I find her with my hands and duck down over her.

Trees and bushes whip against the car as it speeds down the hill. One of the windows shatters. Bits of glass land in my hair and scrape the backs of my arms. The car goes weightless again when it hits a divot, then crashes back down. Ripley yelps and so do I.

Finally, the car meets something it can't crush in its path, throwing the both of us into the back of the driver's seat.

I groan from the pit of my stomach and try to open my eyes. Saliva is thick in my mouth. A searing fire torches my throat. The world is composed of blurry shadows for the brief seconds I manage to open my stinging eyes. Glass shards press into my palms when I prop myself up on the seat.

Sheriff Cory is moaning and slurring, "shit, shit, fucking bitch," and I know I have to get out, get out, get *out* before he can get me himself.

I fumble around for the door handle—still locked—but the window above is shattered. I push my backpack and then myself through, and crumple shoulder-first onto the forest floor.

I manage to stand, but Sheriff Cory stumbles out of the car before I can get Ripley. My backpack tumbled down the incline after I pushed it out. I go for it and the hatchet, and trip on the uneven ground. I land hard on my hip.

The sheriff's blurry shape wavers toward me. He snarls something garbled along the lines of "fucking" and "bitch."

My fingertips touch a branch. I grip it and slam it into his knee. I'm weak, uncoordinated. It glances along the outside and I think, *Oh shit.* But then he trips on his own feet and falls back through the open driver's side door. His head makes a watermelon-on-concrete *thunk* when it hits the doorframe. He moans and lies stunned.

I haul myself up and grip the driver's side door by the open window.

His whole body jerks when I slam the door on his head. I slam it and slam it until he isn't a person anymore, until the man he once was is reduced to a red smear of meat dripping into the underbrush.

I throw up until I can't breathe. My whole face is wet with tears and snot and saliva.

The lukewarm water bottle he had in the cup holder helps to clear my eyes. The creek at the bottom of the hill we careened down is even better. I stick my head in, think vaguely about parasites, and gargle until my throat is no longer on fire.

Getting Ripley in is more difficult. She's confused and squirming, and panics when I dunk her in the deepest part of the creek. I shush her and spill water cupped in my palm over her eyes and snout until she can blink sad what-the-fuck-mom eyes at me without rubbing them with her paws.

We sit on the creek bed—me staring into the water, her trying to sit on my lap. I wrap my arms around her middle and lay my temple on her back.

"Well," I say, focusing on how her ribs contract under my cheek. "Damn."

There is nothing in this universe that cannot be classified as either a cause or an effect.

Are you at cause for your own life? Or are you at effect?

Speaker at Ascent's Discovery Weekend
Saturday Dinner

CHAPTER 7

Sheriff Cory is no longer Sheriff Cory.

What used to be the thing that contained the emotions, the memories, the experiences of the man is now . . . mush. My brain chooses to show me cherry cola slushy sucked through a straw. If I drew it, I'd have to use cheerful, almost cartoonish colors. I gag and breathe through my mouth.

Ripley creeps up to smell him. I shoo her away.

This is the point that freaking out is appropriate, right? Killing a *human* is prime panicking material. He was a living, breathing person who had family, and feelings, and maybe a pet that loved him.

I am not freaking out. I'm not sure I feel anything at all.

Warmth has already started to leech out of his body. So it's not that bad to feel through his pockets if I don't look at him. I come away with his keys, a crumpled Starburst wrapper, and an iPhone. I breathe in through my nose and out through my mouth and swipe up to make an emergency call.

My thumb hovers over the 9. The goblin inside my head

whispers, *Don't. You killed a cop. You call them and they'll kill you too. They'll shoot Ripley. You need to run.*

Usually, the goblin's suggestions are the opposite of rational. In this instance he's right on the money. I just smashed a cop's head with a car door till he died. It didn't matter that he'd just murdered a man in front of me. It didn't matter that he was literally abducting me. *Filming* cops has ruined people's lives. Killing one? Forget about it. I'm as fucked as fucked can get.

I can see it now: my picture splashed across the news, followed by a screenshot of every time I angry-Tweeted about the cops harassing my neighbors, the words "trailer park" said again and again like a jail sentence.

"Murderer," they'll say to the camera. "Trailer trash," they'll whisper to one another when they think they're alone.

Ah. Yes.

There's the panic. There's the band of iron wrapped around my chest and the fear sinking its claws into my throat.

It ends up being a moot point when the call won't connect.

A warning message pops up when I try 00000 as the password, and then again with 12345. I try his fingerprint, but that doesn't work either. Face ID is *definitely* out. It's difficult to resist the urge to smash the phone with a rock to get at its insides.

"You a serial killer, or what?"

The corpse doesn't answer, but Ripley does look up from the log she's smelling. Her eyes are still bloodshot. My fingertips tingle, and I realize I'm not breathing so well.

What'll happen to her when I'm arrested? Emma's apartment doesn't allow dogs. My mom can't . . . she just can't. The truth is that Ripley will be taken to a shelter where, from the moment she walks through the doors to the second the needle punctures her vein, she will be afraid and, most of all, she won't understand why I'm not there.

I take slow breaths. In through my nose, out through my mouth. Eventually they shift from shuddering gulps to something almost normal.

It takes a few hard pulls to get the passenger door open. There's a dent near the handle and a crack in the window. Sheriff Cory's gun tumbles out of the car when I finally manage to open it. It takes less than a minute to put the safety on while I'm handling it, check the chamber, and see how many rounds I'm dealing with.

The one that went through Clarence was the only shot Sheriff Cory got off. There's sixteen left in the magazine. The handgun goes on the dash while I sit and riffle through the glove box in a search for . . . something. Something to help me. Something to tell me why he did this, and what "this" even is. Out comes a locked pair of handcuffs with no key, a car manual, a wrinkled yellow bandanna, and three crumpled candy wrappers with melting chocolate smeared on the insides.

Something shiny falls out of a pile of random receipts and crumpled papers. It thumps heavily in the footwell and settles against my shoe. It's dark. The thing is surprisingly heavy when I pick it up. The legs are needle-sharp, and prick at my skin. It's metal, green-black and smooth.

One special thing, my brain supplies.

It's a cicada . . . or a cicada pupa? Whatever it's called, this little metal thing is a perfect representation of what's left behind after the thing inside crawls out.

A shrill sound splits the air. My hand closes reflexively. When I open it, there are pinpricks of blood where the cicada's feet pierced my skin.

Hungry, the goblin in my brain says.

Weird, I say back.

Sheriff Cory's phone is lit up and ringing where it lies on the center console. There's no name, just a string of numbers with a central Ohio area code. I drop the cicada and put the phone to my ear.

"Where—you?—supposed to—her—a schedule, Cory."

The voice is annoyed. It sounds like it's coming from a long way away.

"Can—hear me? Come—Sh—backwoods service! Sh—"

There's a beep, and the call ends. Service lost.

My breath is coming quickly, despite feeling like I can't breathe at all. The sheriff was taking us somewhere. He was taking us *to* someone. Maybe several someones. Was the caller referring to him and Sheriff Cory as "we"? Or the two of them, plus others?

Every podcast I've ever listened to about abduction and trafficking and partnered-up serial killers explodes in my brain like an overfilled water balloon. Leonard Lake and Charles Ng killed people together. Kenneth Bianchi and Angelo Buono abducted women and girls as a pair.

Ripley sets her head on my knee. She looks up at me, patiently waiting for me to scratch under her chin.

I'm out of the car and swinging my backpack on before I can think too much about it. The phone goes in my pocket. I pull the holster off the sheriff's belt and clip it to my own.

Something weird is happening on my face. I can feel it, but I don't know what it is until I trace my fingers along the Joker grin that's taken up on my lips. It's not a happy smile. It's certainly not a good one. It's the sort of thing that happens when you're so scared, so utterly fucking terrified that the wires in your brain irreparably twist and you can't do anything but laugh.

I am *so* going to prison.

Ripley is looking at me with her tail tucked and her ears back, and I realize I've been quietly laughing to myself as I buckle the holster.

"Sorry." I crouch to hug her close. "I'm sorry. I'm fine. Everything's fine. You wanna go for a walk?"

Her tail wags once, twice. I take her leash in my hand and steel myself.

"Just a little walk."

CHAPTER 8

It shouldn't be difficult to get to Clarence's house and, subsequently, his landline. The sheriff hadn't gotten more than a few minutes down the road before the car went careening through the trees.

I make the mistake of trying to wipe the sweat on my forehead away. The scrapes that weren't stinging before certainly are now. The back of my hand is light pink with diluted blood.

If only Ellis could see me now. I can just imagine it: him watching news coverage splashed with my bloody, frazzled face.

"Can you believe I let her keep her job? She's a cop killer. Entirely unboneable."

Not that the likelihood of boning was high. It's just nice to be considered, is all.

I drop the leash and let Ripley trot ahead. Now that we're not in a stranger's house she doesn't need to be by my side. Ripley glances back with her mouth wide and her tongue lolling. The image is so immediately funny that for a second it overwhelms the unending dread of the moment.

I stop when we come upon a small cleared area. There's a firepit and a wooden bench facing the creek. A well-worn path leads from the firepit up the slope to what must be Clarence's backyard. How many times did Clarence and his wife walk this path to sit by the creek? How many times did he do it on his own before I walked into his home and got him killed?

I shake my head, take Ripley's leash in hand again, and begin the trek up the path. When we reach the top, I have to lean against a tree to catch my breath.

"That wasn't fun," I say to Ripley, clutching my chest.

My heart is thumping a quick rhythm against my rib cage. She grins up at me, tongue lolling, and for her I guess it was pretty fun.

I stop at the tree line to peer out at Clarence's yard. It's quiet, or at least as quiet as it can be with cicadas shouting their song in my ears on a constant loop.

The picket fence is low enough that I can lift Ripley up and set her on the other side. The first touch of my hand on the back-door handle is salvation. The fact that it doesn't open is hell. It's locked. Of course it is.

Shit. Okay. That's fine. Life in a trailer with a crappy sliding door has prepared me for this exact moment. I slide the edge of my hatchet into the bottom seam between frame and door. It gives a plastic creak when I rock it. There is no "good" quality when it comes to sliding doors—just shitty and less shitty. This one is less shitty. Still, it pops open the fourth time I shift it in its frame.

The landline rests in its cradle in the living room. I'm half expecting it not to work when I pick it up. Wouldn't that just be my luck?

The dial tone is so surprising, I can't hold back a crow of "Ha!" when I hear it.

I know I'm supposed to dial 911. That is the best, smartest thing to do. That's what my internal Emma would advise. Instead, my fingers start to tap out my mom's number.

Before I can finish, I stop.

She doesn't know this number, which means the likelihood of her answering is basically nonexistent. An unknown phone number, to her, is the equivalent of Schrödinger's debt collection agency. Even if she did, it's not like she can *do* anything. She'll just be stuck in Columbus scared and unable to help.

No, this is a bad idea. I know it's a bad idea. I should call 911. I dial Emma's number instead.

She answers immediately. "This is Emma."

"I'm in trouble."

There's a pause, then, "Lou?"

"Like really big trouble. I'm fine. I mean, I'm alive. Ripley is alive. But I fucked up."

The landline is rattling against my ear, and I realize it's because my hand is shaking.

"Lou, I want you to take a deep breath, okay?"

My lungs have been shooting out short, staccato breaths

that have gone straight to my head. I blink past the fuzzy-brained feeling and take a second to breathe in sync with Emma.

"Okay. Now tell me what's going on."

I do. I tell her about the coyote; about the hole drilled in my tank. I'm rushing to get the words out, so I don't know if I'm even making sense—not that any of this makes sense in the first place. The last thing I tell her is Clarence suggesting we call the sheriff.

"Are you calling me from the station? I can be there in like two hours to pick you up."

My face is hot and wet, and oh shit, am I *crying*? Why am I crying?

"Lou." Her voice is stern. She's not angry at me, but she *is* angry. "Where are you?"

"I'm at Clarence's. The sheriff came. Cory. He said he wanted to take me to the station. We were about to go and Clarence was gonna follow, but then the sheriff shot him."

The last part is a whisper. Like it's so absurd, so horrific that it can't be said at a normal volume.

"I was already in the car. He drove off and I kind of freaked out. We crashed and I ran."

I stop there because it's the bad part. It's the part that might make her stop being my friend.

"What happened to the sheriff?" Her voice is strained, which makes sense.

"I . . . I slammed a car door on his head until it was mush."

Silence, and then Emma's hoarse voice breaks it. "Dude, what the fuck? Like, literally, what the fuck?"

I sit on Clarence's couch and let Ripley jump up beside me. I can see the driveway from here. There are other people involved in this whole situation. If they come, I'll see them.

"And then I went back to Clarence's, and now I'm calling you."

She's quiet.

"You think I'm crazy?"

She mutters, "Well, there is a certain precedent." She gathers her words in the following silence. "No, I do not think you're crazy. First things first: fuck that cop. I'm glad he's dead. Second: you need to hang up and call 911, okay? You call, tell them why you're out there, that someone sabotaged your truck, you wound up at Clarence's, and then someone killed him and tried to abduct you. You got away and locked yourself in the house. You don't fucking tell them it was the sheriff. It was just some guy. Do you understand? You don't tell them it was a cop."

A wave of pure relief flows through now that I have someone to take control; to tell me what to do. Every single muscle in my body relaxes. I sink bodily into the couch, and Ripley leans more heavily into my side.

"Okay. I can do that."

"Ask for them to send the fire department. Lie—tell them the last time you saw your truck it was smoking or something. Tell them you're hurt and need an ambulance. Just try to get someone other than the cops there. I'm leaving right now, okay? Do you know the house number?"

I tell her no, but she can follow the directions to the address I sent, then give her a description of Clarence's house.

"Try to call me when they get to the house. I'm going to call my professor. He'll know a lawyer."

"What about Ripley?"

She pauses. There's rustling, then a door opening and closing. She tells me to hold on while the phone switches to the car's Bluetooth.

"Honestly, I'd leave her at the house. They're not going to let her in a hospital and we don't want the cops to get their hands on her. Put her in a bedroom or something. Leave a few bowls of water, maybe some food, if there's anything she can eat, and a note explaining she's friendly and it's an emergency. I'll pick her up. If I can't, I'll figure something out."

The thought of leaving Ripley in this house, of leaving her *behind*, makes my stomach gurgle.

"Can you text my mom? Let her know I'm okay?"

Emma pauses again. This time it's longer and quieter than before.

"Did I lose you?"

"No, sorry. Don't worry about that right now, alright? The only thing that matters is getting you somewhere safe. We'll deal with everything else after."

"Yeah. Okay."

Normally, that'd be a monumental task. I can't remember when I started measuring my decisions by the metric of how they'd impact my mom. Maybe because I always have. Will it help her? Will it hurt her? Always in my mind. Always the deciding factor.

But right now? When my current circumstances have hurtled *far* past monumental into the territory of colossal? I can manage it.

"When you hang up, you'll call 911, right? Right away."

"I will. Right away."

I don't want to hang up. I don't want to sever the connection to normalcy. I want to keep listening to the whiny feedback from the car's Bluetooth speakers. As long as I do, nothing that bad can happen, can it?

I dial 911 as soon as the call ends.

Two beats and a woman's raspy voice answers. "911. What's your emergency?"

This might be a massive mistake. I just planned this call with Emma. What if it *sounds* like it's been planned out? I need to sound like I'm scared.

You are *scared,* Emma says in my head.

"I need help. I'm in Russell Township on Harmon Road. A guy just tried to kidnap me. He shot the man who was helping me. My phone isn't working and I can't get any service. I don't know what to do."

"Ma'am, what's your name?"

"Lucie Moore."

"Lucie, you said you're in a house. Do you know the number?"

"No, no, I don't know. It's—There's only two houses on this road. It's older. There's a deer statue by the road. The man who lives here—his name is Clarence. He was really nice. I think he's dead."

"Are you injured, Lucie?"

I look down at myself. At the dirt smeared across my jeans, at the puffy red patches where the world has scraped against my skin. I almost say no, then remember.

"Yes. I need an ambulance. There's a lot of blood. My dog is with me. She got pepper spray in her eyes. That's probably pretty bad. I don't know. She's friendly."

"Thank you for telling me, Lucie. Authorities have been dispatched to your location. I want you to stay on—"

"I need an ambulance!" Ripley whines. I'm yelling. I quiet my voice and stroke Ripley's head nervously. "Not just the cops. I said I think Clarence is dead, but I don't know. If he isn't he needs an ambulance like right now."

"They're on their way. Can you see him?"

"No. He's outside."

"Okay. Stay inside and stay away from the windows. They'll help him if they can when they get there. Can you tell me about the man who tried to kidnap you? Do you know where he is?"

"No, I don't know. Middle-aged. White. Brown hair. Blue eyes." Inside my head is a buzzing, blank space. I hope I'm doing a good job. I hope she's not just sending the cops. I hope they don't shoot my dog if she does. "Do you know when they'll get here?"

Moving toward the bay window is a bad idea. I know that. It pulls at me anyway.

The 911 operator's voice comes from a distance. She's

asking if I knew the man who shot Clarence or if he was a stranger.

Blood stains the collar of Clarence's flannel and his neck. Dark-colored splatters mark the grass around where his body lies crumpled in the yard.

Was that in him? I think numbly.

Coagulation, my brain supplies.

What if he's alive? The side of his face turned toward the house is undamaged. The only sign of injury is the blood itself. It's too far away to see if he's breathing. What if he is and I'm staring uselessly while his life seeps out into the ground?

What if—

His hand twitches. Maybe I'm in shock and seeing things. Maybe I'm projecting what I want to be true onto the situation. Or, maybe Clarence is still alive and his hand just moved.

"I have to go outside. I think he's moving."

"Ma'am, wait for the—"

"I won't hang up, but I have to go outside. If he's alive I have to help him."

"Don't—"

I don't hear the rest. I lay the phone on the ground and open the front door.

Terri: In 2014, a post appeared in r/AskReddit by user WhatsGrapening. The title: "Strange photos found on a camera in lost-and-found box."

Naomi [gasps]: Oh my God, did someone find his camera?

Terri: For everyone listening, Naomi has literally grabbed my arm, she's so excited. [muted sound of movement] Here's the pictures. OP's dad worked at the Columbus Conference Center. Over the years, he collected items from the lost and found. One of which was a camera—Jamie's camera. One of the commenters saw the pictures and connected it to this case.

Naomi: Shit, you really dug.

Terri: I really dug. We'll post these on Instagram, everybody, don't worry. The first picture taken at the retreat is of a group of a dozen people. Jamie is at the front and he's holding a sign that reads "ALR 2001!!"

Naomi: What's that stand for?

Terri: No idea. The *R* might be retreat? The next ten or so are pictures of the area. Trees, flowers, and a bunch of bugs. The eleventh shows a group of five people standing with their arms on each other's shoulders on a trail. Jamie is the last on the left.

Naomi: He looks happy.

Terri: Yeah. They all do. Okay, so, I want you to zoom in on the trees over Jamie's shoulder. A few commenters pointed something out. I can see what they're talking about, but I don't know if that's, like, because they suggested it.

Naomi: Okay. [two beats] What . . . is that?

~~~~~~~~

Lovely Dark & Deep: Missing in the Woods Podcast
~~~~~~~~

CHAPTER 9

Gristle and gore that wasn't visible from the window becomes immediately apparent as soon as I get close. The thin skin of Clarence's face and the white hair on the right side of his head are painted with blood. There's a crevice in his skull. Everything that was once kept safe inside is now spilling out.

It feels like a violation—almost lewd—to be able to see inside a person's skull. Illustrated, the scene would be in color with his head replaced by a cloud of black scribbles. The blood on his clothes and the grass would be in grayscale. It's too private, too intimate for color.

Ripley inches forward to smell his shoulder. How many dead bodies does your dog have to interact with before you're certified as a bad dog parent? If it's three, I'm fucked.

There's something happening in the cavern of my head. A swarm of bees has moved in where there used to be a brain. This is a man—a man who was kind to me. Who tried to protect me. Because I chose to come here today, he's gone. Didn't he say he had a daughter?

Just as the weight of what happened to this man begins to settle, a car tears down the road. It passes the driveway before I can even think to duck or hide or run toward it to ask for help. A dust cloud lingers in its wake.

The car's crappy brakes squeal when it comes to a hard stop on the gravel road. There's a beat, another. And then it reverses just as fast as it drove by.

My instinct is to flee, so that's what we do.

We'll go inside, lock up, and put something in the sliding glass doorframe so it can't be bypassed. I called 911. We'll hide. It'll be fine.

Or it would be, if the front door would open. But it doesn't. Clarence knew he was leaving. He must have locked the knob. I didn't check before we went outside.

The car is in the driveway now. A few seconds and they'll see us.

The shed at the side of the house. We run for it. I fling the door open and we duck inside.

Immediately, I trip on something and thud to my knees. It's dark, but I can still make out the vague shape of a workbench. Shadowed lumps that must be tools hang on the opposite wall. Humid heat wraps a death grip around my throat.

The brakes screech again, this time much closer. Two car doors slam shut.

I scooch until my back is up against one of the workbench

legs. Ripley immediately tries to sit on my lap. I push her off in case we have to run again but keep my arm around her so she can't wander.

People are talking. Yelling, really. The yelling gets closer.

Ripley squirms. I tighten my hold.

"—whole thing has been a disaster! I said it would be. No one listens to me. No one cares what I've got to say about anything!"

"Calm down, *Greg*. You don't need to yell."

"Calm down? Are you for real? This is not a 'calm down' situation!"

Ripley's ears twitch like tiny satellite dishes. She tries to move away again. I dig a treat out of my pocket and hold it in front of her snout. She noses at my fist, suitably distracted, and I thank my compulsive habit of stuffing dog treats in my pockets.

"The sheriff is *dead*; there's another dead guy on the lawn; and we have no idea where she is! I will not be calm, *Leah*!"

Greg says her name with disdain that can only exist with familiarity, then keeps yelling.

"We need to figure out our next steps. We can't be split up like this. It's not smart! Why is everyone so stupid. We have to stick together and find her."

There's a drawn-out, pointed silence. Greg asks, *"What?"*

"Can I FT you?"

"Now? Seriously?" A pause. "Fine."

"Thank you." Leah does not sound like she's thankful at all. "It's not your role to question the plan. It's your role to support it, and to trust that what happens is what is supposed to happen. You're choosing to have a stressful experience. Choose something different."

"Okay . . . harsh. I'm not questioning it. I just think—"

"Stop thinking."

"I just—"

"If you keep on this path," Leah says, voice hard, "I'm going to have to bring it up in a session. For your own good. Emotional parasites need to be purged and, frankly, you clearly have a big one."

It's quiet again.

"You don't need to do that." Greg sounds small. Maybe even scared. "I trust the plan. I do. I apologize."

"No apologies—"

"—only change. Yeah." Greg clears his throat. "Can we check out the house? Being next to the woods gives me the heebie-jeebies."

"It's perfectly safe." Suddenly, Leah's voice is much closer. "Let's open the shed first. I want more people with us when we go through the house."

I scramble toward the handle. I get to it barely a second before it turns. Maybe from her side, it feels like it's locked or jammed.

There's a moment of charged silence.

"There's—"

I throw myself into the door and collide with the two people who are standing on the other side. We all go down in a sprawling pile.

Leah's on her back, gasping, the air knocked from her lungs. She's white and older than me, possibly in her late twenties, early thirties. Maybe I shouldn't be surprised by her appearance, but I am.

I guess I was expecting a version of the sheriff. White, older, angry, radiating internalized misogyny. Not a millennial wearing Chaco sandals and a shirt with a pride rainbow on the chest pocket.

I try to get up, then fall flat with an "Ooph!" Greg's hand is wrapped around my ankle. I kick and connect with his head. He digs his nails in. I kick out again—miss. My thoughts go pinball wild. I'm caught. Hooked in a bear trap. I can't get away.

Everyone thinks their dog will protect them when something horrible happens. They imagine a robber breaking in and their best canine friend chasing them out of the house. Nine times out of ten, that is not the case.

It's not the case this time either, but she *is* a scary-looking pit with a deep bark, and sometimes that's enough.

Ripley lunges, barking at his face. Greg lets go to throw his arms up reflexively. I manage to get to my feet, then crank my leg back and land a five-star punt against his jaw. His head snaps to the side. He stays down.

I grab Ripley's collar and pull her with me toward the tree line. It's just in time too, because Leah is working her way up to standing, her hands in her pockets, searching.

The sound of a Taser kicks up just as we breach the tree line. Leaves slap against my face, and I trip over fallen branches. We run. I tumble down the hill, fall to my knees, and run some more. Cold creek water splashes my thighs. I flail on algae-covered stones, then clamber up the bank to the other side. Mud squelches between my fingers and leaves my legs streaked with brown.

The underbrush is thick on this side of the creek. Running turns into stumbling after Ripley down one deer trail to another. I go until I can't breathe—until my legs shake and I have to brace myself on a tree to keep upright.

It's when I let myself slide down the trunk to the ground that reality truly sinks in.

There are people, not just some corrupt cop or a stranger stalking me for fun, but multiple people trying to kill me and I have no idea why.

CHAPTER 10

I don't know where I am exactly, but I do know that if I keep walking due south I'll hit a county road eventually.

And so we walk.

And walk.

And trip on roots hidden under detritus; and get caught on bramble thorns; and just keep putting one foot in front of the other until I'm pouring sweat and the sun is slowly creeping across the sky.

Ripley sticks her snout in the second creek we come across. She holds it under, then jerks back with a loud sneeze. Dogs are so weird. She got chased by a rabid coyote, tossed down a hill, and pepper sprayed, and barked at a weird guy. It took her about half an hour to bounce back.

I, on the other hand, haven't been able to stop my mind from barreling from one explanation to another. My newest and most boring theory: drugs.

A backwoods narcotics operation with a sheriff on the take is far from the most convoluted thing I could think of.

Two cops were caught in Columbus transporting fentanyl just a few years ago.

Assuming a white person wearing a pride shirt wouldn't associate with a sheriff is pretty naive of me, if I'm honest with myself. I've been to Columbus Pride. It was very clear just how far white queer people are willing to go in order to support the police. After whiteness, money does tend to be the strongest uniting factor.

Regardless of the who or the why, the most important thing is to keep moving. Emma's on her way. She might have even called 911 herself. I can easily see her convincing whoever had the misfortune of answering to send a full fleet of firefighters.

We just have to keep moving.

Which is much easier to say than do. I used to think of myself as a hiker. I think I might just enjoy a nice little walk. This off-road shit sucks.

The suck level increases when the terrain begins to change. Less light makes its way through the canopy to the ground, which has taken on a moist and lightly spongy texture. Screaming frogs in the distance rival the hum of cicadas in the air.

After a few more minutes of walking, we come across a crime scene.

Clumps of fur litter the area. It's on the ground; clinging to the bark of an oak tree; stuck to a muddy, melon-sized rock. Soft clumps of undercoat rest like tiny fairies on ferns. Animals fight. Animals die. This isn't just a raccoon who got into a tussle and left bits of its coat behind. It's everywhere.

One silver tuft appears to be floating in the air a foot or so above my head.

On second glance, it's not floating at all.

Dozens upon dozens of those things that were on the gate hang in the trees like fucked-up Christmas lights. The crosshairs are secured to brown twine that snakes through the branches in a long, seemingly endless line. How far would I have to walk before I found the end? If there's an end at all. It could be as perpetual as an ouroboros. As endless as this crappy day.

Hollow wood chimes dangle from most, but not all, of the crosshairs. It's enough that the gentle *tock, tock, tock* is near constant.

The fur that looks like it's floating is snagged on one of the bundles of twigs.

Why would someone do this *Blair Witch* bullshit?

One of the crosshairs has fallen to the ground. I crouch to get a better look. It's a mirror image of the three that hung from the gate.

My knees pop when I stand. That's not weird; joints do that sometimes. What's strange is that it's the *only* sound in an otherwise silent landscape. Birds don't call or move through the trees. The scream of frogs is gone. There's not a rustle or the soft sound of wind in the leaves.

There are no cicadas. Not one buzzing, not one flying. None.

And I don't see Ripley.

She hasn't been more than ten feet ahead the entire time. She couldn't have gone far. I take a breath to call her name, but I can't make myself break the silence. The woods have decided to be quiet. There's probably a good reason for that.

A soft rustling comes from behind a tangle of bushes up ahead. I pick my way from stone to fallen log to exposed ground, avoiding noisy twigs and brittle leaves.

The smell comes first. It's the thick, decomposing scent of spinach two weeks past its best-by date with a wisp of sweetness I can't place.

Behind the tangle is a natural hollow that, at one point, was carpeted by ferns. Now, their plant-corpses cover the ground in a rough circle maybe twenty feet in diameter. Liquid, dark and shining, slicks the ground. A black crop circle cut into the trees.

Dark masses varying in size are scattered through the hollow. Some are small as a fist, and others have the size and slump of a raccoon bloating on the side of the road. All the darkness—on the ground, on the mounds, on the ferns that haven't yet fallen—blends into itself.

It's eerily similar to the kill scene in the meadow. Too similar to be a coincidence. And this black gunk . . . Much of the coyote's fur, where the skin underneath *hadn't* been stripped from its body, was coated in something dark. Maybe it's whatever's currently seeping into my boots.

One of the masses twitches, and I swear, I *swear*, it cocks its head to look at me, which is impossible because its ribs are exposed to the air and nothing can be alive when it's torn up like that.

The maybe-twitching corpse isn't even the most interesting thing in the hollow.

In the center of the dead earth sits a box.

The box sits on a trailer meant to be pulled by an ATV. The trailer's bed is bowed in under the box like the spine of an animal pulled down by a swollen, pregnant belly. Divots in the earth, obscenely wide and deep, mark where it was dragged.

The box itself is square and made of dark brown—nearly black—wood. Metal bands wrap around the outside. They're thick and burnished dark by age. Something is etched into the metal bands. It's too far away to see clearly. A vague outline remains of something circular that used to be painted on the side. It's not large. No bigger than the width of my hand. Most of it has been washed away. Sun-bleached.

The door—the mechanized kind meant to let pets outside—is raised. Inside is a deep, impossible darkness.

There's a new sound. It's meatier than the drone of cicadas. More of a hum. I'm not sure if it's coming from the box or from inside my head.

The soft rustle again, this time to the right. The hum falls away as soon as I look away from the box.

Ripley emerges from twiggy bushes and living, knee-high ferns. The pure relief of seeing her is short-lived. She's not looking at me. She's not looking at anything. Her gaze is unfocused and her head is hanging low. Everything about her is slumped.

I kneel in front of her. She doesn't react. Not when I say her name quietly. Not when I cradle her head in my hands. Her cheeks and snout are wet.

My palms, when I pull them away, are stained black.

I know it's a mistake to bring my hands up to my nose, but I do it anyway.

I gag at the slimy spinach smell and press my mouth to my shoulder to keep from throwing up. Wiping my hands on the spongy earth clears most of the goo away.

The dregs of my water bottle go to cleaning the gunk off her head. She sways through all of it. Still not really looking at anything.

I'm crying when I finish, because I don't know what this gross shit is, but it's clearly making my dog sick and the blisters on my feet sting and I got some off her, but not all of it and I don't know what to *do.*

The forest is being quiet, which means I should be quiet too, but Ripley is acting strange and I can't stop crying and shivering and there's humming in my head again and—

And in the mess of the thoughts, one is very clear: *I feel weird.* I think the black goo is *making* me feel weird. Is this shit toxic?

Something moves in my peripheral vision. I wipe at my teary eyes with the back of my hand, realize my mistake, and use the inside of my shirt instead.

There. Something just moved behind a tree.

I stare so hard at it that my eyes sting. There's a hatchet wound of discoloration across the trunk where naked wood has been exposed to the world.

A low, weak growl vibrates in Ripley's chest. She's gone whale-eyed, and her hair is up all the way down her back.

I look back to the tree.

The discoloration has separated into four distinct fingers. The hand falls from the bark and vanishes behind the trunk.

Icy fear snakes through my veins and freezes me in place. I'm a rabbit that's caught sight of a predator. I can't move, can't breathe, can't think a single thought other than, *Don't let it see you*. And then just like a rabbit, I bolt.

Ripley is limp as a bag of bricks when I scoop her up. I hold her to my chest with one arm under her ribs, the other under her butt, and run. Branches whip my cheeks and sweat stings my eyes. A log nearly sends us down when I trip on it.

The sound of someone crashing through the woods follows us. Don't look; just keep running—if what I'm doing can be called running. I should have grabbed the sheriff's gun from the holster, but my hands are full and Ripley's so heavy that my feet drag more and more, and then they're right behind me, and I can *feel* them reaching for the back of my shirt, and—

We break through the trees onto the shoulder of a dirt-and-gravel road.

Scattered gravel slides under my boot. I flail and land in a lunge, one knee slamming onto rocks. I squeeze my eyes shut, fully expecting whatever's pursuing us to smash into my back.

A beat. Another. After a third, I stand, then turn slowly. I don't know what I'm expecting. What I find is nothing but trees and *dozens* of crosshair chimes hanging from branches and nailed to their trunks.

I can't look away. It feels like I just trespassed through

someone's yard and hopped the fence just in time to escape the guard dog trapped inside.

Shivers run through my body like I've got a fever. Everything aches. I think both me and my dog are high or poisoned, or both. The idea of sitting down and not moving for a while is becoming more and more appealing by the second.

And then one of the trees shifts.

Except it's not a tree at all. A figure taller than any person I've ever seen looms between two close-set trunks. It's mostly hidden by sucker branches and cast in shadow by the canopy. Dappled sunlight falls on an emaciated hand dangling by its sharp, bony knee.

There's a pit in my stomach. I have an overwhelming sense of déjà vu that I know the figure like I'd know a bloody tooth pulled from my own mouth. The hum that began when I looked into the box gets louder. It feels like someone's holding a tuning fork to the base of my skull.

Ripley weighs so much, but I think if I set her down I could go to it and—

Only once gravel shifts under my foot do I notice I've taken a step forward.

I tighten my arms around Ripley despite shaking from the strain. I could go to it and do *what*? Abandon my dog? Leave her by the side of the road so I can touch whatever weird fucking thing is staring at me from between the trees? No.

Something is wrong. It feels like there's something in me that shouldn't be there.

There's an odor. A scent so thick I'm swimming in it. Something is—

burning, burning, my skin is

burning. Something is on—

fire where it touches

But there's no smoke. No—

screaming and screaming and screa—

I'm so focused on the tree line and the smell and the *burning* that I don't notice the car speeding around the curve until it's far, far too late.

Terri: You see it?

Naomi: It looks like . . . Have you seen *The Blair Witch Project*? This is *Blair Witch* shit.

Terri: That's what I thought too! For the listeners: if you zoom in on the trees on the right side behind Jamie, it looks like three brownish circles hanging from the branches. You can zoom in on some of the other trees and find similar circles, but the ones behind Jamie are the clearest. Okay, next picture. This one really got me. So, the camera is focused on a green tree frog on the side of a tree. The background is partially out of focus. If you look to the left . . . you see behind that tree?

Naomi: No. No. Oh, I really don't like this.

Terri: It is out of focus so you can't 100 percent make it out, but it looks like there's someone crouched close to the ground. It's kind of blurry like they were trying to hide, but weren't quick enough. A few redditors say it's just a light flare or dust in the camera lens—

Naomi: Dust? Girl. That's a fucking person. Is this real? Like it's not photoshopped or anything.

Terri: I think it's real. The last eight pictures are taken at night. It's a mix of blurry trees and bushes, and then these ones [pause] which are pointed straight up at the sky through the canopy. The last one is from the forest floor, like Jamie fell or the camera did. This one is the blurriest. You okay?

Naomi [voice thick]: I just . . . Imagine being lost in the middle of the woods, it's dark, and you can't see where you're going so you use the flash on your camera. How is this not more well-known?

Terri: I keep asking myself that exact question. We've covered a few cases that aren't widely talked about that really deserve to be. This one is just . . . It's that last picture for me.

Naomi: Like, what happened to Jamie that it ended up on the ground?

Terri: Exactly. I can't stop thinking about it. About how scared he must have been, you know?

Lovely Dark & Deep: Missing in the Woods Podcast

CHAPTER 11

A hard jostle jerks me awake.

Opening my eyes is a mistake. The world spins and spins and the only way to make it stop is to close them and take slow breaths through my nose. There's grit in my mouth and a chemical cleaner taste on the back of my tongue.

"Hey, kiddo. Take it easy, alright?"

That voice. I open my eyes a sliver because I *know* that voice. Ellis is looking at me from the driver's seat of his car; his face is blurry yet somehow still concerned. Relief is a wave that washes through my body, followed closely by another intense urge to throw up.

I scrabble to unbuckle the seat belt before I hurl all over myself and his car, then yank the door handle. It's locked.

"Whoa, whoa!" Ellis says. "It's okay. You're safe."

I gag and slap a hand over my mouth, trying to keep the hot rush of bile inside. He catches on and unlocks the door. I'm falling out of the car as soon as the locks click. There's nothing in my stomach to throw up but a throat-scorching mix of water and stomach acid. I heave until I'm panting and tears stream out of my eyes.

A door slams and gravel crunches. Jeans and hiking boots stand in my peripheral vision.

"Here."

Ellis holds out a handkerchief. I take it and blow my nose. He hands me a second handkerchief. I don't know why it's funny, but it is. I huff a laugh and wipe at my eyes. Who carries a handkerchief? Let alone two?

The world is still swirly, but not as bad as it was. I take deep breaths and try to figure out what's going on.

We're still in the woods, but on a road. No looming monsters in the trees. No crosshairs either.

"I am so sorry." Ellis crouches next to me. His hands hover over my body, like he's afraid to touch me. Makes sense since he just hit me with his fucking car. "You hit your head when you fell. Probably a concussion if the vomiting is any indication."

Sure enough, there's a wet spot on the back of my head. Even the slight brush of my fingers over the pulpy skin makes me catch my breath.

"Where's—" I clear my throat. "Where's Ripley?"

"She's in the back."

I try to stand, but the waves in my head slosh and roll. An involuntary groan pushes out of my mouth.

"You can take your time—" Ellis stops when he sees my face. "Okay."

"No," I want to say. I have to see her. I think if I open my mouth again all that'll come out is another groan.

Vertigo has me clutching his arm as soon as I'm standing. It takes an embarrassing amount of effort to peel my fingers from his biceps when it passes. Even more embarrassing is how grateful I am that he continues to keep a steadying hand on my back.

Ripley doesn't respond to me opening the door. I put a hand on her side. It takes a moment, but she lifts her head to look at me. My stomach drops. It's clear she's doing her best to look at me. Despite that, her eyes roll in their sockets and her eyelids drift down.

She flops her head down like the effort of holding it up even a moment is just too much. There's something under her nose. More black gunk? I use one of the many loose, crumpled napkins in Ellis's car to wipe it off.

It's not black. It's red.

A sob gets stuck in my throat. I don't know if the blood is from the car or that black crap, but either way it's bad. This is so, so bad.

This time the sob makes it out of my mouth just fine.

"I'm so sorry," Ellis says. "I shouldn't have been going so fast. I was rushing."

"It's not just the car. She got something on her. It was this black . . . gunk. I was cleaning it off when I got scared and we ran. I thought . . ."

Remembering the thing in the trees makes my stomach flip.

"What?" Ellis asks when I look to the tree line.

I don't see anything. I don't hear anything. That doesn't stop the persistent feeling that if I reach my hand out, I'll touch it. Whatever *it* is.

"It's unfortunate." He speaks slowly, carefully. "But illegal dumping is common out here. Some of it is extremely toxic. In combination with something internal from the car . . ."

What we found in that hollow didn't feel like a by-product of industry. How it felt, how it *smelled*, was of decomposition and rich, dark dirt.

Regardless of what it is or where it came from, we need to leave.

I tell him so and he says, "No kidding. We need to get you to a hospital."

We're going to an emergency vet first. That discussion can wait until we're back on asphalt. I indulge in feeling Ripley breathe under my hand, then let Ellis help me back into the car.

"Why are you here?" I ask.

He reaches over me to buckle my belt. Before, this would have been thrilling. Now, I'm just tired.

"You never called. I tried your cell but it didn't ring. The property owner has a trail camera on the gate. I asked him to check and he said your truck was still there. It was a slow day." He shrugs. "I thought I'd drive down to my cabin in Hocking Hills for the weekend. Decided to pop over to check on you on the way. Hit you with my car instead. I'll probably have to throw my '#1 boss' mug away when I get back to the office, huh?"

"I'll buy you another one if you can get us out of here. I tried to leave, but my truck wouldn't start. And then . . . everything just kept getting worse."

"You are having a rough day." Ellis squeezes my knee. "Hey, want to drive?"

He jangles the keys in the air. He laughs at whatever face I'm making. "Joking. Extremely joking. You shouldn't be walking, much less driving."

It's a terrible joke, but it does make me choke out a watery laugh.

"Lou." His face is serious, and then he's cupping my cheek. He leans in close and meets my eyes. "You have done so well. I should have never sent someone down here alone. This is my fault, not yours. I've got it from here. I've got *you*."

The words don't process. My brain literally can't make the idea of someone *having me* compute. Sometimes, when things are very bad, I'll daydream about an alternate life where the moment I turned eighteen I got on a bus and never looked back. My mom doesn't call. I don't have a dog. Not even a houseplant. The only weight I'm carrying is my own.

Reality floods in every time.

Maybe I'm not a woman, but I *am* a daughter, and being a daughter is its own horror story. The walls are splattered with blood and guilt and righteous anger and, most important, love. Horror is nothing without love. The weight of it stoops my back until I'm curled in on myself like some fucked-up fiddlehead fern.

Something I've never been proud of and that feels almost

impossible to admit is that, honestly, I don't want to be strong enough to carry my weight and someone else's. I want to be rescued.

"You're safe now. I'll keep you safe. Okay?"

He shuts the door and moves around to the driver's side. Relief is instant the moment the car gets going.

"How'd you know where I was?" I ask.

"I didn't. This is the only other road near the property. Figured I might as well check."

The rearview mirror shows Ripley lying on the back seat. If I focus, I can see her breathing. Ellis is such a pack rat. There's junk everywhere. We go over a particularly large pothole. The pile he must have shoved over to fit her on the seat shifts.

The shift reveals a box of loose Ascent trifolds. The only reason I don't roll my eyes is because it'll make me throw up. I wonder how the leaders at Ascent Discovery Weekend would make this my fault. Something about negative energy attracting bad actors, probably.

I close my eyes to block out the scenery moving by outside. That makes the dizziness worse, so I focus on the handle to the glove compartment instead.

A wordless, voiceless whisper brushes against the shell of my ear. I flinch away from it like a dog from a fly.

"What is it?" Ellis asks.

There's no one in the back seat but Ripley. I look forward to the glove compartment, and ignore the feeling of a hand hovering just above my shoulder.

"It's nothing. I'm fine."

"You don't seem fine, if I'm honest. Can you tell me what's going on?"

I hesitate. What if he doesn't believe me? On the other hand, how is he supposed to help me if I don't tell him what I need?

"Someone drilled a hole in my gas tank while I was on the property. My phone wasn't working, so I walked to one of the houses on Harmon. The man who lived there, Clarence, called the sheriff. Sheriff Cory."

I take a long, slow breath. "The sheriff, when he got there, he said he'd drive me to the station. Clarence was gonna follow us. But the sheriff—he shot Clarence in front of the house. We were already in his vehicle. I didn't know what to do, so I used my pepper spray. We crashed. I walked back to the house and called 911."

We come to an intersection. The perpendicular road is asphalt—old and cracking—but asphalt all the same. Every second we're getting closer to a vet and away from this property. Soon the feeling that a specter is trailing after me will go away and everything will be fine. I'll never have to think about something too tall and looming watching me from behind the trees again.

"Also, there was a rabid coyote on the property. It chased us. I haven't seen it since."

He shoots me a look as though *this* is the part that's surprising. Wait until he hears about the maybe-monster. That is, if I decide to tell him.

"Huh." He's quiet for a moment. "Did you talk to anyone else?"

Ellis is not smiling. He's frowning. As soon as he notices me noticing, his expression goes back to concerned. There's something perched on the tip of my tongue. It's a song I know the tune of but not the name.

"I'm not criticizing you. I'm just trying to get the full picture. This is *a lot* to process."

Try living it, I want to say. Instead, I motion to the water bottle in one of the console cup holders. "Can I?"

"Of course! Please do."

Half the water is gone in a few swallows. Once I'm done, I breathe through my nose to curb the urge to throw it all up. I try to put the bottle in the cup holder closest to me, but there's something in it already. What I pull out is the same dark black as the interior of the car.

A small, stone cicada.

"Neat, huh?" Ellis says.

I don't say anything. I can't. All the pieces of information I've tacked up in my brain are connected. I just couldn't see it before.

It's the way that Leah and Greg spoke. Phrases like "emotional parasites" and acronyms like "FT," Frank Talk.

It's the way that, when we spoke this morning, Ellis said he'd be in constant meetings, but just now he said it was a slow day.

It's the box of brochures in his back seat despite him telling me he'd never taken a class.

A beat. Two. Ellis unspools. His back goes from straight to relaxed. His left hand drops from the steering wheel to his thigh. His posture says he's never been touched by tension, never been overcome with anxiety once in his life.

My hatchet—

Is in my backpack, which I am no longer wearing. The holster is snug on my belt. The gun, however, is gone.

My eyes burn—not from tears but fury. I didn't even think to check if the gun was still there when I woke up.

I lay my head back on the headrest and watch the canopy move by through the sunroof.

"Smooth."

"Thank you. I wanted to be a magician when I was a kid. Sleight of hand, distraction, the works."

"I wanted to draw comics. How did you know where I was?"

He's smiling. "I've got trail cameras all over the property."

There's anticipation in his silence. He's leaving an opening for me to jump in with questions and accusations. He wants me to ask so he can tell me. No one loves a story more than Ellis. I don't ask. He says it anyway.

"This would have been so much easier if you behaved like a normal person. Who chooses some hick's house instead of the nice one next door?"

Click, click, click goes the turn signal, and then we're back on Harmon Road.

Branches scrape against the car. The sound covers my seat belt unclicking. This isn't a cop car, so unless the child locks are on, all I have to do is press one button to get out.

Ellis *tut*s. He reaches down between his seat and the

door to bring up the gun. It rests on his thigh with the muzzle pointed at me.

"None of that."

We pass Clarence's place. I don't look in the yard.

Click, click, click goes the turn signal, and then Ellis is pulling into the driveway of the new-construction home I chose to pass. That I was *right* to pass.

Three people emerge from the front door as soon as the wheels touch the driveway. Two men and a woman. All white, each wearing bloodred scrubs. I recognize the woman and one of the men. Leah and Greg.

Greg's nose is swollen and covered with a bumpy gauze bandage. The third is older. Late fifties, white and the sort of tan that lets everyone know he went on vacation this year. He could be any one of the businessmen with two-hundred-dollar haircuts walking around Downtown Columbus.

Ellis puts the car in park.

"Was it real?" I ask. The need to know is overwhelming now that we're stopped. "That thing in the woods. Was it real?"

Ellis turns his handsome face to look at me. The gun on his lap, a soft smile on his lips. "I don't know what you're talking about."

Greg and the guy who I've decided to call Haircut approach the SUV. Haircut opens my door. Moist summer heat and the drum of cicadas roll over me. Haircut smells like the on-sale cologne kids buy for their dads on Father's Day.

Ellis lifts the gun in an out-of-the-car gesture, then sends a look back at Ripley.

"You behave and we'll take good care of her. If you don't . . ." He shrugs.

Slime, says the goblin.

The tendons in my jaw itch with the urge to bite down, to *eat him*.

I flinch, making him smirk. I'm no stranger to violent thoughts. But this animal urge to *eat* him? I don't know where it came from; I just know it wasn't me.

Haircut puts a hand under my arm to help me out. I think he might have a chance at being charming if I knock his teeth down his throat. *That* thought is 100 percent mine.

An arm wraps around my chest from behind, and a wet cloth is smothered over my nose and mouth. I inhale, startled. Mistake.

My mouth and throat are flooded with the familiar smell of chemical cleaner.

The cicadas stop singing. My limbs go numb. The world shifts. I'm not falling; I'm being lowered.

The last thing I see is Ellis looking at me from above, one corner of his mouth quirked.

CHAPTER 12

Chloroform doesn't work the way movies say it does. You'll wake up in a few minutes unless the rag stays on or is put back repeatedly.

That's why when I surface enough to find myself lying flat on a hard surface with voices drifting in and out around me, and they bring out the rag *again*, I know that I'm probably going to die. Doctors stopped using chloroform to knock patients out years ago for a reason. Sometimes they just didn't wake up.

I fade in and out to hands on my skin, cool air blowing over my face, the tidal motion of being lifted and carried. Voices, always voices, speaking around and over me. A rag is pressed to my mouth for the fourth, maybe tenth time.

And then, finally, I surface for real.

I blink up at buzzing fluorescents and ceiling tiles, then throw myself to my side to hurl up everything I've ever eaten. What comes up is nothing but water and stomach acid. I clear my throat and spit onto the carpet, then lie on my side. I lie there, drifting, until the drum pounding away in my temple can't be ignored.

I go to touch my temple and stop short. My hands are bound. Cuffed together. They're so tight that lines have formed under the metal where they cut into my skin. It doesn't feel real, this thing restricting my movement.

It takes a beat to realize why my palms look so strange above the handcuffs.

They're clean.

My fingernails are trimmed and rounded, and my cuticles have been oiled. Any trace of the woods, of the black gunk in the killing field is gone. I hold my hands to my nose, and my skin smells like I've been crushing lemon rinds and sage.

There's a hummingbird trapped in my chest. Its wings beat faster and faster as I push up my sleeves to find bruised but clean skin underneath. And then faster still when I see I'm not pushing up a grimy flannel, but a soft white dress.

The hummingbird propels me off the thin carpeted floor. I don't get far before there's a hard jerk just under my ribs.

A chain, silver and thick, is secured around my waist. It's tight enough to leave marks. The chain, in turn, is secured to a metal plate screwed into the cinder-block wall. The air is musty and cool. I'm in a basement. No amount of pulling or clawing could get the chain free. You'd need bolt cutters—big ones—to make a dent, and then probably not even then.

Trapped, the goblin says.

What comes next isn't a word, but a feeling. A torrent of

feelings of being trapped, unable to move, unable to escape, stuck in the dark—

And then I scream.

If my throat was raw before, now it's bloody. Every thought that isn't *Get out, get out, get out, get it OFF*, pours out of my head. I scream and try to push the chain down over my hips but the—

walls press back, contorting your limbs and trapping you in the dark

If I had something sharp, I could carve away my flesh until it fit over my hip bones. I could carve off my breasts and dislocate my shoulders and gnaw off any bits that were keeping me—

locked in this box

—chained to this fucking wall.

Arms wrap around my chest from behind. *Again.*

A moment of vertigo takes me, and then I throw my unpinned arm back as hard as I can. The crunch of cartilage under my elbow is almost satisfying enough to overshadow the instant pain radiating up my arm. There's a warm rush of liquid on the nape of my neck, and then I'm released. Before I can turn to face whoever it is, I'm thrown on the ground.

I'm being held down by people with faces smudged out by a thumb. They tell me to stop, to calm down, other things that don't make sense. I shriek and kick and tell them to go fuck themselves. One lets out an "Oof!" when I get him in the gut. He presses his forearm to my throat. Footsteps pound down the stairs. Let them come. I'll hurt them all.

Haircut's face materializes out of the blur. The man whose nose I crushed with my elbow pulls away, choking and sputtering blood. I recognize him. It's Greg.

Haircut is in my face, shouting. "We'll kill her! We'll fucking kill her if you don't stop!"

He fists a hand in my hair and yanks. The world goes blurry from the pain radiating from the gash at the back of my skull. A whine whistles out of my lips.

"Look! Just look!"

I do. It's two people—one standing in front of the other. I know one of them.

Her arms are behind her back and she's gagged with a bandanna. A bruise swells her left cheek. Hair has escaped from the claw clip at the back of her head and sticks to her sweaty skin. There's a wickedly curved knife pressed to the soft skin of her neck.

"Emma?" Her name is more wheeze than word.

Haircut leans more heavily on my throat. He's panting. "Are you calm?"

Every tendon and muscle in my body is ready to kick, to bite, to claw. I swallow it down and nod.

"Doing that again would be very bad. Do you understand? We have plenty of sedatives here. Or we could tie you up so you can't move at all. We don't want to do that. We don't want to hurt your friend either. Okay?"

I nod again, tasting the burn of bile in the back of my throat.

He retreats to stand between Leah and the youth pastor–looking motherfucker holding Emma.

"Jesus Christ!" Greg says. It comes out more like "Jeshush Chisht." He glares at everyone around him. "She broke my noesh *again*!"

Leah says, "Calm down."

"Fuck you, Leah. Anyone elshe notishe I'm the only one getting my shit kicked around here? Thish ish sho fucked!"

Haircut orders, "Go upstairs."

Greg flees up the stairs at the far end of the room.

"Rough day for Greg," I say.

"I understand this is very traumatic for you," Haircut says. "What you're feeling right now is understandable. It's valid. Regardless, we're going to need you to calm down and listen to what we say. We do not want to hurt you. I'd rather you be comfortable. But, if you don't cooperate, we'll punish your friend. If that doesn't sway you, consider that your dog is upstairs. We'd like to spare her, but, again, if you choose not to listen, she will die in pain, wondering why you aren't there to make it stop. Is that what you want?"

"How do I even know she's alive? You could be lying."

Haircut nods to Leah. While she's taking her phone out of her pocket and flipping through it, I'm watching Haircut. Who's the boss? Is it Ellis or this guy? Haircut is ordering people around, and they're listening to those orders. Was Haircut communicating with the sheriff? Or someone else I haven't met yet? How many people are in on this?

Leah turns her phone around so I can see the screen. It's Ripley. She's lying on a blanket in a bright room. Her eyes are closed. For one heart-stopping moment I am certain these people are showing me a picture of my dead dog, but the angle shifts, and I realize it's a video.

"Riley," a voice says. A bell rings in the back of my head, then goes quiet. "Hey, doggie, look here. Yeah, that's it. Good dog!"

Ripley opens her eyes. There's a spot of red on the blanket under her snout. She blinks slowly. The video ends.

Leah puts her phone back in her pocket. Her lips are smug, and her hair is in a stupid messy bun that's still the perfect amount of messy despite everything.

Hurt her, the goblin says.

I would if I could—

reach the hand dangling too close to the cage, small bones crack between your teeth, warm blood coats your mouth, the thrashing animal on the other end shrieks and shrieks

My hand goes to my mouth. No blood dripping from the corners. No flesh stuck between my teeth. Still, the ghosts of porous bone and wet meat linger in my mouth.

Haircut looks relieved. "Right now, you just have to wait. That's it. Just sit here and wait. Do you think you can do that?"

"What are we waiting for?" I ask.

"Are you hungry? Thirsty?"

I stare at him. He didn't answer my question, and he's not going to. He keeps the same polite, unbothered look on his face.

"We're going to head out now. Leah will be down—"

"I don't have any money. Don't know anyone with any either. If that's what you want, you've got the wrong person."

Leah huffs and rolls her eyes.

Haircut continues to ignore me and helps Youth Pastor secure Emma to another chain bolted into the cinder-block wall. She jerks out of their grip when the padlock clicks in place, linking the handcuffs around her wrists and the thick, metal chain together.

There is a series of chains spaced out on the white walls that I hadn't noticed. One of which sits directly under a rusted brown stain on the wall.

Haircut motions Leah to the stairs. Before he turns to leave, he says, "We'll be back. Please keep calm in the meantime, okay? We'll know if you don't."

Panic hits me as they clomp up the stairs. What if they leave and don't come back? What if they leave us here and flies lay eggs in our eyes? That strange déjà vu finds me again. This time it's—

panic as they retreat and the meager dark descends; hunger twists and burns and twists and burns and eventually sleep comes but not true sleep and then the light again and the hunger again and the pain again again again

The basement door snicks shut.

Emma stands stock-still, glaring at the bottom of the stairs. She blows air out of her nose like an angry bull, then says something I can't understand through the bandanna. She kneels, and after much wriggling and many angry muffled words, manages to work the handcuffs under her feet. She yanks the bandana down as soon as her hands are out front.

"Wow," I say.

"What the fuck! Like, literally what the *fuck*, Lou."

I hold up my hands. They're shaking, just like my breath.

"I'm not saying I told you so, but I fucking did tell you so. I warned you, dude. What did I say? You were going to be serial-killed." She stands and holds up an angry finger. "You may be thinking, 'But it's a cult, Emma. Technically you were wrong.' I submit the fact that they've clearly done this before to other people. It's a serial-killing cult!"

She motions to the other chains on the wall, then begins to pace as far as the one attached to her will let her go. I don't have words. If I did, what would they even be? She stops and turns to me.

"Why are you wearing an ugly prairie dress from Target?"

Her tone makes the question into an accusation, like out of this whole situation it's the thing she's angriest about. There's definitely something wrong with me, because it makes me laugh. The skin on my face pulls weird and too tight when I smile.

"Maybe it was on sale."

She scowls at me, then slides to the ground. Her arms go around her knees.

"What's going on?" she asks.

All the anger she had before has drained away, leaving a quiet despair I've never seen from her. Despair is infectious.

It's airborne and insidious. When they come for us, they'll crack my ribs and find nothing but dark, despairing air inside.

I draw my knees up too and press my back to the wall. The chain cuts into my middle. I resist the urge to dig my fingers into my skin and tear. I ache all over. Did the person who undressed me feel anything when they saw the bruises decorating my skin? Were they gentle or did they press down on purpose?

"I don't know."

Lou 3:09 pm: they keep asking me about the Ascent weekend thing

Mom 3:49 pm: tell them to fuck off

Lou 4:03pm: i think i might just have to do it to get them off my back

Mom 4:11 pm: 🙄

Lou 4:12 pm: it might be interesting?

Mom 4:15 pm: its a hippy dippy bullshit cult

Lou 4:25 pm: lol yeah i think you might be right

Mom 4:26 pm: i just don't want this
stupid job to change you into a person
you don;t like

Lou 4:27 pm: I like being able to pay the rent. I like you being able to take days off sometimes.

Lou 4:53 pm: *image of latte with foam resembling a dog*
Emma made this for me this morning

~~~~~~~~

Text conversation, July 13, 2018
~~~~~~~~

CHAPTER 13

I know that, logically, there's no dress code for horrible people.

You can't *look* like a serial killer or a sexual predator. I know that, yes, Richard Ramirez, Charles Manson, and sour-milk Ted Kaczynski himself had aesthetics that screamed B-A-D in blinking neon letters. Paul Bernardo and Karla Homolka, on the other hand, could have been anyone's hot, shitty cousins. Look at the horror they inflicted. All of Ed Kemper's cop friends thought he was a goofy, harmless guy. He brutally killed six college students.

All that being said, Leah and Greg don't seem like the torturing, murdering sort. Haircut, on the other hand, probably drowns kittens for fun. As for the man who was holding Emma—I've never met a youth pastor who *didn't* seem capable of killing.

I don't know about Ellis. I don't know why I didn't see the black hole lurking behind his bright eyes and quick smile. Emma's reaction to him is very different when I recount everything from the moment I called her onward.

"I'm not surprised. Horrible people seek out positions of power that let them feel benevolent. I'd put money on most CEOs having actual bodies buried under their patios."

"You just don't like bosses."

She wrinkles her nose but doesn't deny it. Labor girlie, through and through.

"I knew there was something wrong the moment he stopped me on the road. His voice was . . . off. I should have Tasered him. 'It might be dangerous. Let's go together.' Asshole."

"I don't get it," I say after a minute of silence. "Why do any of this? What's the point?"

There has to be a *point.*

Emma worries her hands. "I'm not joking about it being a cult. There's weird stuff painted all over the walls upstairs. People were going in and out carrying chairs and, like, lanterns, I think. Cult shit."

The last two words are said with such finality.

"There were symbols on the gate. The one that led to the property. Circles with a plus sign through them. Is that what was on the walls?"

Her gaze is intense on the side of my face. "There were creepy cult symbols on the gate to the property. And you went through anyway?"

I don't know what to say. My reasoning, which seemed so strong at the beginning of all this, can't stand up to the disappointment and anger in her voice.

"I asked you not to do anything dangerous, right? Didn't I do that? What would make you think, 'Oh I know. I'll walk through the creepy cult gate and straight into the forest'? Why didn't you turn around? Or call me? You had Ripley with you. I thought at least you'd think about her."

The handcuffs jangle when she runs them over her face and through her hair. She slumps. The anger I could handle. The defeat, I cannot.

"I don't— I couldn't lose this job. My mom— I thought it'd be fine. I'm sorry."

Her face crumples. She doesn't answer; won't look at me. I close my eyes and press my palms into the sockets. I can't lose her. I can't fail her too.

This job was supposed to save us—save me and my mom. *I* was supposed to save us.

A shiver licks its way up my arms. The smell of cigarette smoke makes my nose itch. I don't want to open my eyes. I don't want to see it. I *can't* see it. I hold my breath, but the smell is already in me. Tobacco and ash. Cigarette butts and warm beer. My mom started smoking when she was sixteen. She told me when I was in middle school. It was a warning not to follow in her footsteps. She did that a lot: laying out her life like a map of roads I shouldn't take, choices I shouldn't make.

"You're better than me," she'd say again and again. "You'll be better than me."

Sometimes, I wonder if what she gave birth to wasn't a baby at all. Maybe it wasn't anything other than her second chance.

And now, instead of saving anyone or being anyone's

second chance, I've managed to get my best friend chained up in a basement, my dog hit by a car, and my mom—

The ceiling creaks.

I open my eyes. I'm still in the basement. The smell is gone. In its place is a thought—a single encapsulating sentence.

This job was supposed to save us, but all I got was credit card debt, chloroformed, and coworkers who call my dog by the wrong name.

CHAPTER 14

Leah descends the stairs fifteen minutes later.

Emma is a champ at hiding what she's feeling. She'll be unbeatable when she's fighting bosses at a bargaining table. Keeping my face blank is not a skill I ever learned. The gears connected to my facial muscles are inextricably linked to my thoughts.

We talked about this in hushed whispers—about how I know exactly who the person taking that video of Ripley is and, most importantly, about how we need a plan.

Leah carries two small eight-ounce water bottles.

"Stay where you are." Her eyes flit between us. "There's a camera in that corner."

She motions to the backmost corner of the basement. I don't see anything that could be a camera. There's nothing but the smoke-stained ceiling panels and the white cinder-block walls. The basement itself is empty but for the three of us.

"If you try anything they'll know. Understand?"

I nod, though I'm not sure they would. Emma is frowning at where Leah pointed.

Leah stands in the middle of the room, out of reach. She tosses us each a bottle of water.

When we don't move to pick them up, Leah sneers. "Well?"

"I'm not thirsty."

"Me neither," Emma says, stone-faced.

"Being contradictory isn't a personality trait, you know. It's just annoying, and it makes you kind of a bitch." Leah takes her phone out of her back pocket and waves it at us. "We're trying to be nice. One call and your dog's dead, and if that doesn't work a dozen people are going to hold you down and *make* you drink it."

Emma and I look at each other across the room. The fact that she has to call means that if there is a camera, it doesn't have sound.

Emma drinks first. She makes a face. Leah watches her until she finishes the bottle. I consider the water, then take a sip.

It's vaguely salty. No idea what that means. Probably something bad.

I ask, "How's Greg?"

"Better than the sheriff. Keep drinking."

Another sip. Saliva floods my mouth and my stomach gurgles. I take a slow breath.

"It'd take a lot to be worse off than that guy. Hope he didn't want an open casket."

"You know he had a wife? A *kid*."

"And yet he still decided to be evil. That's on him. I have

a mom, friends, a dog. *You* kidnapped me. *You're* the bad guy in this situation. Fuckin' duh."

Leah smirks.

"What's so funny?"

"No, you don't."

"I don't *what*?"

"No. You. Don't." She puts her hands on her thighs, leans down like she's talking to a child. "You don't—"

"Shut up," Emma says. Before she drew Leah's attention off of me and onto her, she managed to creep almost to the end of her chain.

"I said stay by the wall."

"Shut the fuck up." Emma's blank mask is gone, and in its place is panic. "Leave her alone."

Leah laughs. "Holy shit. I forgot. You're crazy too. We put a God View on her phone, you stupid bitch. We read all your sad little messages. What's wrong with you enabling her being crazy like that, huh?"

"You—" My heart is stuttering in my chest, and my head is floating. I can't tell if I'm having a panic attack, or if it's whatever's in the water. It wouldn't be this instant, would it?

"*You*," Leah mocks in a whiny voice. "You don't have a mom. You've got no one. You are no one. That's why you're here. The only meaningful thing you'll ever do is die. You should be grateful."

There are no thoughts, only action. I whip the bottle, spraying the liquid that's left at her face. She steps back and reflexively tries to block it with her hands. I throw the bottle at her face. She takes one more step.

It puts her close enough that Emma can grab her by her perfect topknot. Leah flails, then hits the floor. The sound of Emma's foot impacting her stomach is a thick thud, followed by a choking gasp. Leah curls into a ball on her side and clutches her middle.

The whipcrack sound of a Taser lighting up punctures the air. Emma's face contorts into waves of twitching spasms from the Taser pressed to her thigh. She kneels on the floor gasping for breath.

Leah gets to her feet, still clutching the Taser. She looks like she's about to use it on Emma again, thinks better of it, then abruptly turns to retreat. She gets a few strides in, and then Emma's tennis shoe smacks into the back of her head.

Leah whirls on Emma and lets out a sound of pure frustration. She's still backing up, holding the Taser with both hands in front of her like a sword.

"Did you just throw your *shoe* at me? What's wrong with—"

Leah tries to take another step back, but trips on my outstretched leg.

She stumbles, arms wide. The world slows as she falls, and a thought rings through my head clear as a bell.

Hurting people is actually pretty easy. It's the getting-started part that's hard.

She hits with a muffled "Ooph." The Taser flies out of her hand. I grab her ankle. She jerks away, but I hold on. Her squirming just makes it easier to pull her toward me.

The new thing taking shelter in my skull is panting and shaking and all I can think is:

yes yes YES eat survive

The world falls away until there's nothing but the hot rush of a struggle between living and dying. She's below me. Her nails rake across my neck. I feel it, but not enough to stop me from pressing the handcuff chain into the thin skin of her throat.

Her hand is on my chin, pushing me away. My tongue and lips are slick. Iron in my mouth and at the back of my throat. Did I bite my cheek? Did I bite her? Either way something is bleeding.

This is a bad way to die, I think. *This is a horrible thing for Emma to see.*

I can't do this.

I pull back. I'm shaking so hard that the handcuffs clink when my wrists knock together. Goose bumps cover my entire body. The world is melting and blurring into a swirl of colors.

A whisper of breath brushes against the shell of my ear. It carries the smell of decomposition.

I try to move, but I'm too slow. I'm never fucking fast enough, am I? I'm never fast enough to save myself or anyone else.

A weight slams into my back. It knocks the air from my lungs and presses me into Leah. I can't get up past my elbows, and I can only get a little space between the chain and her neck. My biceps scream from the effort.

"Don't, don't, please—"

All there is, in and around me, is rage. It's not hot, not fiery. It's a frigid Ohio river, running brown and thick with ice in the dead of winter.

Cold hands slide down my shoulders, down my arms, down my wrists. The thing—the monster, because it's not human, it can't be—rests its hands over mine. Its fingers, long and cold and gaunt, worm into the spaces between my own. They're the same fingers I saw at the hollow.

The hands press and press and press until I feel my wrist bones grinding—

together, always together they come to burn you to trap you, they're never alone, this one is alone, this one will die, *they'll all—*

It's not mine. The emotions. The images. None of this is *mine.* The tuning fork has been shoved right in my ear canal, and something slick and wet drags over the wound at the back of my head. A drop of black lands on Leah's cheek, then another. I close my eyes because I can't see this. There's nothing I can do to shut out the sounds—the choking, gasping sounds—

I don't open my eyes when the weight leaves. My skin shivers like a ripple in a pond. I'm on my side, numb, face wet with snot and tears. I don't look at the thing that once contained a human next to me.

The monster's breath brushes over the nape of my neck.

And then it's gone.

Catharsis comes at great risk. What if you escape what has been keeping you trapped? What if you're no longer able to ignore the role you take in your own life? There will be no excuses to hide behind. Only your own culpability.

You put yourself at great peril by crawling from your shell, naked and vulnerable, with the hope of achieving your highest potential.

We see you, we acknowledge you, and we accept you.

Ascent Initiation Script

CHAPTER 15

Emma is throwing up.

I know because I can hear her, but I can't open my eyes. I can't look at what I've done. I can't face how Emma looks at me now that she's seen me kill a person. Hands shaking, I feel along Leah's side until I touch the outline of a phone in her pocket. I take it and move away so I don't have to see when I open my eyes.

I laugh when the phone lights up and opens when I swipe the screen. Lucky.

My eyes hurt from straining to focus on the phone. There's something wrong with me.

It takes hours, years, a century to make the phone work. When I do, I laugh again, triumphant.

I can do this. I can *do* this.

What am I trying to do?

I have to call someone.

I have to call my mom.

No, no, I can't. But why not? I don't remember.

"Lou, the phone." Emma's voice is wet and choked.

I see my index finger dialing her number. It's a path pressed into the earth that I could follow in pitch black. I know it better than my own.

It's too hard to hold the phone up, so I curl on my side and cradle it on my cheek. It rings. The sound lights a stuttering flame of hope in my chest. Emma says my name again. I ignore her. I'm getting help; she doesn't need to worry.

It's good I'm calling my mom now. She'll know what to do.

The line rings and rings and rings and in the background Emma asks for the phone, but I can't give it to her because this will save us, I know it will. The mechanical voice asking if you want to leave a message comes on.

That's fine. She's probably asleep. Bleary-eyed and slow to get her glasses on. It's late. It's so late.

I redial. It rings and rings and then the message again. My heart thumps hard.

One more time. It's the third call. It'll work. She'll answer.

Her voicemail message is an echo, an endless ripple in my head. I want to call again, but my fingers are numb.

Why wouldn't she answer? Why wouldn't she pick up the phone? After it rang once and she didn't know the number, maybe not. But three times? Even from another phone she knows what it means. She *knows* it means I need help.

She always answers or calls me back right away. If she's alive she'd find a way to answer, to get in contact, to—

Oh.

Oh.

If she were alive—

—she'd answer.

My head fills with sloshing waves. I can't breathe. I'm slipping into vertigo. Someone is saying my name. It's not my mom. It's not her.

I blink. I'm home.

The hallway is dim, and the air is stale with the scent of cigarette smoke. The light burned out last week. Every day since I've told myself I'd grab another on my way home from work. Mom doesn't mind, but I do. There's something about a dim house that makes anxiety rise in my throat like bile. A dim house means musty curtains and broken blinds and shadows to hide the trash left on the floor because neither of us had the energy to pick it up.

Today. I'll write it on my hand. One of those Edison ones maybe. Class the place up a bit. Bring some brightness into our lives.

"Mom?" I knock on her door.

Normally, she'd have been up for hours by now. She texted me yesterday that she was going to bed early, so I'm not surprised she forgot to set her alarm. I'd leave without waking her if it were up to me. I'm finally making enough that she can take a day off here and there, but not enough that she won't spend her day off feeling anxious about bills, groceries, and everything else on the endless list.

"Mom?" I wait a beat, then turn the knob.

Ripley wiggles into the darkened room like she hasn't seen my mom in weeks.

The door catches on a pair of scrubs crumpled on the floor. I pick them up and toss them into the hamper. I'll have to put a load in the washer before I leave so she has a clean uniform tomorrow. She says I don't have to do her laundry, but, just like with the light, who's going to do it if not me?

I look to the bed, expecting to see Ripley furiously trying to lick at her cheeks and my mom pushing her away. Instead, I find Ripley standing stock-still on the bed, body curved away from the figure lying under the quilt. Her tail is tucked under her tight.

"What are you doing?" I laugh at her.

I move to the bedside. I put my hand on my mom's shoulder to wake her up.

What my hand touches isn't my mother. It has her silhouette, but none of her warmth. This *thing*—this thing is stiff and cool to the touch. A buzzing sound like thousands of beating insect wings crawls into my head. Spots light up the darkness of the room.

Suddenly, my hand is knotted in Ripley's collar and I'm watching myself pull her out of the bedroom. My mouth is moving, but what am I saying? The words are slurred, blending vowels into consonants, and spilling from chattering teeth.

"—have to leave her alone. Just let her sleep. She's have—having a rough week. Have—have to let her sleep."

My lungs stutter, and my face is wet. Phlegm coats my throat and the inside of my nose. I can't *breathe*. Ripley struggles against me, and I let go when I realize the collar is too tight on her throat and she can't breathe either—

I'm on my knees in the dim hallway, running my hands

over her neck, chanting, "Sorry, sorry, sorry." She's shaking. I'm shaking. I crawl to the bedroom door and pull it closed with my eyes squeezed shut.

She's tired. She has to sleep.

I'll let her sleep. When she wakes up she'll feel better.

The next thing I remember is opening my front door to the police two days later. One of my mom's coworkers called them to do a welfare check when she didn't come in to work.

My memories are liquid after that. Bits rise to the top while others sink to the bottom of a cool abyss. What I was able to gather: I'd found my mother dead in her bed, in our home, had a seismic dissociative episode according to the therapist I went to twice, and then just . . . didn't tell anyone. I went to work. I didn't say a word. I didn't say anything all day long. I kept going to work and coming home until the cops showed up two days later.

While the cop was walking down the hall to my mother's room, I drafted an email to Ellis telling him I had to take emergency leave because my mom was sick, and I didn't know when she'd get better. I don't remember writing this email, but I know I must have because it's there in my Sent folder. I don't remember texting Emma that I needed her to watch Ripley, but I did that too. Efficient and practical, taking care of everything that needs to be taken care of all the way to the end.

When a cop sat me down in an interrogation room, he asked if I didn't tell anyone my mom was dead because I was the one who killed her.

I remember my mouth shaping words to convey that I didn't notify anyone because she *wasn't* dead. I also remember the look on the cop's face—a mixture of pity and disgust—and the urge to smash his face into the two-way mirror until all his teeth tumbled out of his head.

I was so full of rage and so fundamentally unable to process it.

It's just that I thought, one day, if I could just manage to make enough, if I could just *be* enough, show her enough love, give her enough hope for the future, I could heal my mother. I could make up for everything she gave up for me.

I worked and worked and shrank and shrank with every bite the world took out of my flesh like I was some tasty little morsel that existed only to be consumed. One day, I thought, the world will stop swallowing down bits of my body. I just had to find a way to be enough before the world took a mouthful so big I couldn't survive.

They let me go when the coworker who called in the welfare check, Janet, explained why she called in the first place. My mom slipped while giving a shower to a patient. She hit her head on the tile floor. The nursing home's manager had acted like it wasn't a big deal and sent my mom home to sleep it off.

While she slept, her brain bled.

And then she died.

She was probably already dead when I got home from work that night. I'd stayed late to work on a report for Ellis. She was already in bed by the time I walked in the door.

Must have been a long day, better let her sleep, I thought when I found her door closed. So that's what I did.

"Subdural hematoma," the coroner said.

"Criminal working conditions," Emma told me.

"She's sick. She just needs rest," I told everyone who asked.

There's a sound. It's soft, pitiful, and made by something small. It's me. I'm crying,

"Emma, my mom is dead."

My voice is so slurred with tears and whatever was in that water that I can barely understand myself.

She must understand me because she responds. "I know. I know. I'm so sorry. Lou, I need you to give me the phone. I need you to do that for me. *Please* do that for me."

The phone? The phone. Everything is heavy and loose. I'm a water balloon sloshing across the ground. My stomach jumps and I think I might throw up.

Emma's face is wet and her eyes bloodshot. She's already got her arm stretched across the carpet, like it's been that way for a while. I push it toward her. The phone slides, slides, stops just out of her reach.

She makes a frustrated, angry sound and reaches out to it with her foot.

A tentative voice calls down the stairs, "Leah?" just as Emma makes contact with the beaded chain attached to the phone's case.

The voice is unbelievably congested, which makes me laugh. It's Greg!

Greg's talking to another person and the other person is talking back. Emma has the phone to her ear and she's talking too. The only sound that makes sense is the feet thumping down the stairs.

I flop over to watch. There are legs standing in front of me. The legs belong to a man. The man crouches. He's close enough that I can smell the spice of his cologne, feel the intense focus of his stare.

Ellis regards me. He's wearing a crisp white T-shirt while the other people wear maroon scrubs. His hair's in a low ponytail and there's a streak of dirt on his cheek. I think, absurdly, *He looks good.* Smells good too, like pine. It was really nice when I thought he was going to save me.

Emma is yelling, furious and frantic as a hissing cat. Abruptly it cuts off. The room feels empty without her voice in it. No, that's not right. It's not the room that feels empty.

It's me.

There used to be a point to me.

Ellis rests the back of his hand on my forehead. He's warm, and it makes me want to cry.

"Aw, Lou. What are we going to do with you?"

Lou 1:13 pm: Cn you watch Ripleuyy?

Emma 1:22 pm: Of course. When?

Emma 1:23 pm: Are you okay?

Emma 2:13 pm: There are cops all over your house. they're saying it's a crime scene? They won't tell me where you are

Emma 2:41 pm: Fuckers weren't going to give her to me but I got ripley. You need to call me as soon as yo ucan.

Emma 3:13 pm: Please call me.

Emma 9:48 pm: I'm so sorry, Lou.

Text conversation, March 20, 2019

CHAPTER 16

There's a hand on my forehead, and then gentle fingers in my hair.

I'm flat on my back with my hands over my head. Ellis stands over me. His head is framed by blackened sky and white pinprick stars. He's wearing white scrubs and a leather necklace. At the end is the crosshair symbol and a silver dog whistle. Whatever I'm lying on comes up to his waist. The word "altar" comes to mind.

The night sky and his face blend together. Every inch of my skin feels hot and overly sensitive except for my feet and hands, which are cold. No—numb. Something rough and stinging is tied around them. I twist my hands and gasp when rope burns lines into my skin.

"Ah-ah," Ellis admonishes. "I know it's tight. You killed Leah handcuffed and chained to a wall. We're taking no chances."

I shake my head, which is a mistake, because there's still a water balloon where my skull is supposed to be.

It was me, but it also wasn't. The thing stretched along my back was *real*. Right?

His smile is self-indulgent. Warm light moves across his face. It casts him as soft and inviting, like someone who would put his arm around you when you cross the street.

I can't believe I wanted to fuck him.

We're surrounded by lanterns like tiki torches, all strung together by a garland of twine and crosshair chimes. The lanterns form a long rectangle of flickering light that stretches from the deck to about halfway down the yard. Ellis and I are at one end.

At the other sits the box from the killing field.

Someone has brought it here from the woods and laid a path directly to me.

Warm light from the lanterns spills onto the wood. The changing shadows illuminate etchings on the metal bands. Dozens—hundreds of circles, each split into four by crosshairs.

My heart thumps a drumbeat that gets quicker and quicker. Humming and the placid *tock, tock, tock* of the chimes fills my head. Goose bumps spread down my arms. Suddenly, I'm shivering, shaking because of what comes next.

But what comes next? I don't understand. Why do I feel like I'm—

burning, burning if it touches you, the sound comes closer and you make yourself small to fit into the meager dark, the door descends and you watch him, the dream of bloody meat in your mouth—

Ellis pinches the inside of my biceps.

I flinch and look away. My eyes sting like I've been staring at the sun. The humming fades; the shivers and the fear remain.

Ellis. It was Ellis in the . . . memory? It felt like a memory.

He looks down at me with an amused expression. "I'm sure it's difficult to focus right now, but I'd like you to try. It can be distracting. Wonderful craftsmanship, don't you think?"

Even after clearing my throat, my voice is raspy. "What—?"

"The crate. They just don't make them like that anymore."

Again, I look at the box. The door that had revealed an inky darkness inside is now closed.

What's gonna come out of that? Don't you wanna see? Don't you wanna know?

Don't you wanna crawl inside and join all the delicious dark things that've walked in, been *pulled* in before you—

I pull my gaze away. I didn't notice the folding chairs set up like pews on either side of the lanterns. Ten, maybe fifteen in total.

Ellis taps my forehead. "Eyes over here, kiddo. It'll suck you in if you look at it too long. Scramble your eggs . . ."

He trails off. The quiet stretches. He wants me to ask. The need to talk, to unfurl his knowledge for someone, drips from him like sweat. There's always a reason behind awful people doing morally bankrupt things. It's the same one again and again: they're special and that specialness means they have the right, no, the *obligation*, to make the special decisions and to be considered the most.

Bullshit. Tell it to the mirror.

When I stay quiet, he blurts, "It's a god. The story about my great-great-grandfather is true. He did save the baron's daughter, but not from a collapse. They dug too deep. When the god crawled out, it went through the miners like a Sunday brunch buffet. He saved her and trapped it. As soon as they realized what having it around did, they started feeding it. Been in the family ever since. The tradition was to let some poor bastard loose in the woods and let it hunt. It became a spectacle." He shakes his head. "I'm proud to say I've modernized. We're not barbarians. You get more flies with honey than vinegar, as the saying goes. The only time it used to see the sun was during the hunt. Now, it gets two full days of freedom to stretch its legs and chase critters to its heart's content. We establish boundaries, of course. Some of which you saw."

He looks to the crate, then grins down at me. "It almost got ya, didn't it? Can you imagine? The sacrificial lamb gets eaten *before* the sacrifice?"

There's something happening in my chest. It's not my heart thumping. It's not my stomach sinking. It's a ghost pepper pushing its way up my throat. My gums and the muscles in my jaw are on fire. The only cure is to *bite.*

"Where's Emma? My dog?"

"You just had to keep on walking." Ellis continues like I didn't say a word. He picks up a lock of my hair and rubs it between his fingers. "I hope you don't think this was all me. Arden hates you so much. Between you and me she doesn't handle failure well. She tried so hard to recruit you. I think it really damaged her. The failure."

Having it confirmed that, yes, it was her on the video of Ripley hurts in a way I didn't expect. For so long, I tried to be the best employee and most pleasant coworker possible. I wore kitten heels and tucked in my shirts and spent a thousand dollars on Arden and Jena's worthless self-betterment cult. None of it—none of it—could cover up who I am at my core. Arden smelled it on me the moment we met.

Turns out that no amount of perfume can cover up the stench of the working class.

This is all so ridiculous. I want to laugh. Of course a personal-development cult has trapped me in the woods so they can sacrifice me to their weird god that crawled out of a hole. Of course they have.

It'd make too much sense for some transphobe to sabotage my truck. Way too pedestrian to wander into a drug trafficker's territory and get shot for it. No, what ultimately does me in *would* be the silliest thing imaginable.

And here it is: the silly thing has come to eat me up. Not only me, it's gonna swallow my best friend and my dog whole too.

"Knew it was a cult."

"It's a cult that *works*." Ellis's mouth is doing something that's less a smile and more a manic grimace. "Humans at the height of actualization are naturally driven to create a better, more ethical world. Do you have any idea how much land I've saved for conservation all over the state?

How much our members have given to charity? Every new Ascentian is a soldier in the Empathy Revolution. Every revolution needs a leader."

The capitals on Empathy Revolution are loud and clear. In a few months it'll be on T-shirts and tote bags and hashtagged to death. Not only will the revolution be televised, but it'll be trademarked too, if Ellis has anything to say about it.

"I have to ask. You had no idea about me, did you? That's on purpose, of course. If people saw what was controlling the hand of God, there'd be no faith, don't you agree?"

Every word drips with zeal and smugness. Again, he pauses for me to react. I close my eyes since I can't cover my ears. "Sure. Whatever."

Silence. Reluctantly, I open my eyes. At least his grin is gone.

"You're not the least bit curious what you're dying for?"

"You sacrifice people in exchange for prosperity. That's just capitalism, and that's been killing me my whole life. It *did* kill my mom." The tears are immediate. I blink rapidly to clear the prickle at the corner of my eyes. "Grow up."

He shakes his head. "My ancestors, my father, did it for wealth. For a spectacle. We aren't—I just *told* you how it's different."

Even his rants about mountains and ancient glaciers carving through the earth don't rival the wide-eyed zeal that's taken over his face. "You don't know anything about power. About *ritual.* I'm changing the world. I'm saving it. All it costs is one person that no one will even remember."

Bone-deep tiredness pushes a sigh out of my mouth.

"I get it, okay? You are a *very* special boy."

A full minute passes with nothing but the sound of cicadas filling the air. He looks up at the darkened sky, then squints down at me. "Arden was right. You deserve this."

Without another word, he retreats into the house.

He's got Haircut and Youth Pastor with him when he comes back. They hold a struggling and still-handcuffed Emma. Blood is smeared across her cheek and her hairline. Her shirt is drenched with sweat. She's 130 pounds soaking wet, but she's still managing to make both men strain with how hard she's throwing herself around.

Haircut and Youth Pastor walk her forward and force her to her knees. I crane my neck, but it's difficult to see with the lanterns between us and the ropes holding me down. Our eyes meet. I know what I'm expecting: anger, fear, disappointment. Instead, she wears a blank mask. She meets my gaze, then looks away.

"Well, alright." Ellis smiles. "Might as well get to it."

Arden: Do you mind if I—

Ellis: No. I'd prefer the takeaways to be more accurate.

Arden: Okay.

Ellis: Where did we leave off?

Arden: The initiation.

Ellis: Ah yes, the initiation. Obviously, I'll lead it. It should be natural, yes? It's a *return* to nature. It should feel very rural. Bucolic.

Arden: Right.

Ellis: Southern Ohio, I think, don't you? It's where it was found. Not at the family property. A new one.

Arden: Okay.

Ellis: The initiation on the first night, and the offering the next day. A Friday and a Saturday, maybe. Tidy. It's a new tradition. We're not some old fogeys going on a fox hunt. That's how it used to be, you know. Let the offering loose, a little chase for the initiates, then throw it to the big guy, watch the show. Profit. Not anymore. We're civilized. We don't *want* to do it, but we have to for the betterment of us and the world. It's not fun. It's not supposed to be. There are two sacrifices: the offering, and our innocence.

Arden: Right. Okay.

Ellis: You've said okay three times in this conversation. You might want to make that a goal. Addressing verbal parasites. You're absolutely capable of it if you actually commit.

Arden: I—Yes. I didn't notice. You're right.

Ellis: I know. That's why I said it. [laughter] The crate should be there. I want them to see it. We'll go over the origin: how my great-great-grandfather trapped it, the molten lead, the inscription, how the company mark evolved, the abundance and tradition that followed, et cetera, et cetera. Do you think they should get tattoos?

Arden: A tattoo?

Ellis: Yeah. A crosshair tramp stamp. [laughter] It'd be appropriate. It wasn't anything at first. Just how they marked the product. A symbol. The symbol gained power, as symbols do. The same concept. The longer we have them, the more they're ours.

Arden: Indelible.

Ellis: Indelible. Yes. Anyway, we've got a few more years until it wakes up. What do you think about that? I don't think I like it. Having to wait for it to decide to wake up. And so infrequently. We should probably control that too, don't you think? Make the feedings more . . . robust.

Arden: Do you think that'll help with its—?

Ellis: Its *what*?

Arden: I wasn't trying to— In the photos it looked like it used to be a little more . . .

Ellis: That's interesting. After viewing a few photographs, you think you can diagnose its condition. That's very interesting.

What do you think the source of that assumption is? Pride? Ego?

[Prolonged silence, the sound of quick walking]

Getting back on track: the feedings should be more robust and more frequent. Repetition reinforces reliance, don't you agree?

Transcript, March 3, 2008

CHAPTER 17

The cultists trickle in one by one.

Each wears the same short-sleeved, maroon scrub shirt and drawstring pants. They look like they've been dipped in wine. Somehow their white limbs came out unstained.

There are twelve not counting Ellis and the two standing on either side of Emma. Greg walks in. He has an even bigger blocky white bandage across the bridge of his nose and a scowl on his lips. A few of the others occupy a familiar, vague spot in my memory: a tall, older woman with willow-thin wrists; a balding fortysomething man with dyed brown hair and an oval face; the young woman who sat at the registration table at the Ascent Discovery Weekend. It's not her face that ignites the spark of recognition, but the clay honeybee earrings that dangle all the way to her collarbones. My memory of her is mixed with the glossed-over feeling of freshly printed pamphlets, coffee poured from carafes, and the hum of dozens of voices introducing themselves.

When Jena walks out, her eyes flick down to meet mine, then jerk up like a dog whose leash has been yanked. Even in the dark the flushed points high on her cheeks are visible. A sickly sweet and alcoholic scent wafts off her. Is she drunk? I'd probably get wasted too if I was about to sacrifice my coworker.

The holder of Jena's leash follows a few feet behind. Arden makes eye contact immediately. How else could she impress upon me the shitty little smirk on her pink-painted mouth?

The humming in my head grows louder. I'm not even looking at the box. There's so much hatred and rage in me. I allow all that hatred to pull my lips back till I'm baring my teeth. Some of it's mine, but most of it isn't. Most of it's—

bite her claw her slash her

rip her limb from limb

Arden looks away. The goblin laughs. I laugh too. This is it. *This is it.* This is the world about to eat me just like it ate my mom. It just so happens that the mouth belongs to a sorority princess who never once got my dog's name right.

"You stupid cunt," I hiss. "You stupid, evil fucking cunt!"

She stops when I start yelling, eyes wide. The cultists sit stunned. The older wispy woman puts her hand to her mouth, aghast and so terribly offended.

"No one will ever love you. You're *rotten*."

Ellis produces a roll of duct tape, then tears off a strip. I snap at his hand when he tries to put it over my mouth and catch a bit of skin between my teeth. He tries again. This time it sticks to my lips and fills my head with chemical smells.

I keep thrashing. Every movement hurts, but it doesn't matter. All I care about is hurting him.

A gun fires. My ears ring, my head rings, my entire body is a throbbing bell. Ellis holds the gun aloft with the muzzle aimed at the tops of the trees.

He speaks directly in my ear.

"If you so much as twitch, I will shoot out your knee. You make a sound, I'll crush your fingers with a hammer. I'll do the same thing to your friend. Do you understand?"

Reluctantly, I nod.

"Great. So glad we could have this talk."

Ellis puts the gun somewhere I can't see. He takes down his hair and looks up at the sky while he twists it into a bun. By the time he's done, his costume of easy charisma has slotted back in place. He levels his gaze at the crowd and smiles.

"Please sit. Let us begin. Thank you all for being here tonight. I am honored to share space with each one of you. I am aware this ritual has not gone as we planned. As we all know, if there's no struggle, then you're doing something wrong."

He smiles and the cultists smile right back, some nodding. He goes on like that. Words fall from his lips in a well-practiced cadence. He talks about sky-puncturing mountains being whittled down by wind and water into rolling hills and the men who ate tunnels through the earth until they reached places that were never meant to be touched by the sun.

I wish I could pet my dog before she dies. I want to hold

her and tell her it's alright, that she's good and I love her. I want to listen to Emma rant about unions and labor law and watch YouTubers laugh about reality shows neither of us have ever seen. I want to do anything other than listen to this entitled, delusional man preach to a bunch of other entitled, delusional people.

I crane my head to see Emma. She's slumped forward, eyes on the ground, hands pressed to her mouth like she's about to throw up.

"The men loved their god," he says. "They fed it, and prayed to it, and honored it every thirteen years with the joy of ritual and sacrifice. In return the men were blessed with prosperity."

He pauses to scan the crowd. They are enraptured.

"The world is different now, and we are not those men. Our needs are larger. Our god demands more. Just like us, it is hungrier. We understand better than anyone that great progress demands great and frequent sacrifice."

Ellis pulls a stone cicada from his pocket, then places it where my bottom two ribs meet. Its sharp little feet pierce through the prairie dress and prick my skin.

One special thing, my brain supplies.

"Please bow your heads." He raises his voice and lifts his hands high. "We offer this sacrifice in supplication. We call you to us—"

He looks right at me. "The god of appetite!"

"The god of appetite!" the cultists repeat.

Ellis reaches down to something I can't see. There's a soft mechanical *snick* from the box when the mechanical door opens. Ellis raises the whistle to his lips, blows once, and then silence.

The whole world takes a breath. Even the cicadas stop their song.

The monster is here.

No, I remind myself. Not a monster at all.

A god.

CHAPTER 18

First comes a hand.

It settles softly, almost tentatively in the grass. The pale fingers flex, then dig themselves into the sod. I'm reminded of hands gripping flesh, fingers digging into necks and forearms, of bruises and abrasions, of the god's hands entwined with my own, cutting off Leah's airway.

Hand over hand, the god pulls itself from the pitch-black mouth of the box. Pale gray, nearly white, forearms emerge, and then elbows too sharp to be human, and then the top of a head that gleams in the lantern light with black, inky liquid.

The god rests in the grass with its head hanging low, its shoulder blades flared like wings above.

Does it breathe? Is it catching its breath? Its back is flexing and contracting, so it must.

It's this—the sight of the clever machine that is a body working—that makes my throat seize. This isn't imaginary.

It's not a hallucination; it's not whatever manifested itself in the basement. This is a tangible body made of flesh and bone and muscle. It's real and it's coming for us.

The god's head snaps up.

It has no eyes. There wouldn't be any, would there? This thing came from a deep, dark place that wasn't meant to ever be touched by light. It has a gash stuffed with sharp teeth for a mouth that stretches from ear to ear.

The god straightens from its prone position on the ground. It's tall—at least eight feet—and thin in a sharp and angular way. Though there are no eyes, I feel its gaze on my skin and in my head. Its teeth hover over the pulse point in my neck despite it being thirty feet away. Hot breath breaks over my skin. There's no looking away from the inhuman thing that's caught me in its fist.

The god's presence ripples through the cultists on either side. They tilt away as it makes its way down the aisle. I understand. The closer it gets, the stronger the tuning fork at the base of my skull vibrates.

The crosshairs sway, and the ones with the hollow pieces *tock, tock, tock* delicately. The god doesn't flinch, not outwardly. Inside, I feel it recoil from the sound.

Being restrained doesn't stop my body from trying to make itself small. It's an unconscious movement born in the same instinctual corridor of the brain where horror and reverence are housed. I didn't need to see this thing take down prey to know it's a predator. The hair rising on my neck and the sweat coating my body tell me that.

Its feet thump on the steps leading up to the deck. One, two, three, and then it's here. The god is here, towering above me.

It's pale like something you'd find under a rock, with oily black smears marking its limbs. Scars litter its skin, mostly in pairs. The culprit: the stick Ellis held in one of the memories. A cattle prod. A few of the scars are sloppy asterisks. Bullet wounds. The worst are the two ragged crosshairs branded into its belly. A foul smell bleeds from its body. It's the raccoon that got trapped under our trailer's skirting until its bloating body burst, releasing the smell and alerting us to its presence.

Pools of shadow form in the contours of its skull; the craters of its collarbones; the ravines formed by its expansive ribs. Ellis said they feed it more now than ever. And still it looks like a starved dog left to rot in its cage. That doesn't make it any less terrifying. A sick lion might not be able to take down a buffalo, but it could sure as hell destroy me.

One of the cultists lets out a quickly cut-off whimper. The god shifts its attention toward them, revealing the source of the smell.

Black liquid leaks from open wounds on the jut of its shoulder blades, the back of its arms and elbows, and on the sharp knobs of its spine. There's even one on the back of its head. I've seen similar in the nursing homes where my mom worked. Bedsores. Wounds where the—

skin presses to wood, to iron, you try to uncurl, try to twist, the only way to move is in, to shrink and shrivel and wait

It turns to me again. Its attention is a wet snail dragging

its body up the tops of my feet, the length of my calves, across the tender skin of my thighs, my navel, the meeting of my ribs, to the squeezable expanse of my neck. My breath hitches, then comes out shuddering.

"A sacrifice given in supplication," Ellis says loudly. "Blessings returned tenfold."

Ellis pulls out a long, vicious knife from somewhere. The gleam in his eyes is just as vicious and twice as maniacal. He raises it in both hands until it's extended above his head.

This is it, I think. *This is it.*

There's a commotion behind the lantern barrier. Ellis's attention shifts to the rising voices. I want to look, but I can't tear my attention away from the god.

The god itself is statue still. There's a twitch at the corner of its mouth so subtle it might have been nothing more than the light sitting odd on its craven body. But then its mouth grows until it's a grin as sharp as the killing blade itself.

"Keep her still—" Ellis starts.

There's a wet squelching sound, and then the sort of silence that's attached to a moment so incomprehensible no words fit around it.

A figure lurches into view. Youth Pastor's neck is slick with blood turned black by the night. His face is slack with surprise. His hands hover around the wound, so I don't see it at first.

Embedded just below his jaw is half of a metal claw clip.

Ellis cries out, "Don't—!"

Too late. Emma darts forward and shoves Youth Pastor

with both hands. His arms go pinwheeling. He falls backward into the lanterns in a cacophony of breaking glass and wet choking. Sparks like orange lightning bugs explode from the shattered lanterns. The smell of kerosene fills the air.

There's a second, just one, where the god stands still, and Ellis is frozen in uncomprehending fear.

And then it's carnage.

The god moves like a striking snake—headfirst and fast as hell. It hits the first person—a middle-aged white woman in the closest chair—and sends her sprawling to the ground. Her strangled scream is cut short by the god slashing her jaw off with its clawed hand. The god falls on another person. This one makes a horrible wet sound when those claws are plunged into their back. Its frenzied elation grows stronger with each kill.

Ellis blows the dog whistle again and again, but it doesn't work. He's shouting about the lanterns and crosshair symbols, about staying calm, about remaining where they are, but the cultists are scattering and screaming and falling over themselves to get away. The fear on his face feels good. It makes me want to laugh.

Ellis remembers the forgotten knife still gripped in his hand. He raises it once more and shouts, "Stop!"

The god's eyeless face turns on him. Meat dangles from its mouth—red and raw and dripping.

A pot full of calendula cracks against the back of Ellis's head.

He drops the knife. I flinch, certain I'm about to be

impaled, only for it to embed itself in the dark wood of the altar an inch from my skin. Ellis clutches his head and disappears out of my view, though I can hear him groaning.

Emma's eyes are wild. She picks up the knife, still handcuffed, and saws at the rope holding my wrists above my head.

Fire from the broken lanterns has spread across the brittle summer grass. Shapes move inside the smoke. A man shrieks, "No! No!" and then says nothing at all. Another shouts, and then something squelches. I follow the god through the smoke by the sound of a person realizing they're about to die and then the wet sound of their body being pulled apart.

The rope comes loose. I sit up and work on unknotting one ankle while she cuts at the other.

Suddenly, Emma gasps and looks down.

Greg lies on the ground with Emma's leg clenched in his fist. There's so much blood on him. That can't all be from his nose, can it? Then I see the wound on his shoulder. Yellow fat and white bone stand out from the red mess of muscle and tendon.

Greg starts to say something. He stops, looks down at his feet, and then he's ripped away. There isn't time for him to scream before the sound of his bones breaking fills the air.

Frantically, we get back to work on my ankle ropes.

"The rope! The rope! Cut it!"

"Shit, shit, shit—"

I slide off the altar as soon as the ropes come loose, then immediately lose my balance to numb feet. Emma grabs my arm and helps me stand. We careen through the patio doors, clipping the frame as we go.

I yank the doors closed. They're the French kind with too many windows and billowy sheer curtains. The spot where Ellis was kneeling on the deck is empty. I didn't see where he went. Didn't see him get pulled away by the god either.

Plumes of smoke choke the yard. There are no more moving shadows. No sounds of death—there's just the dead and the smoke and the god hidden somewhere within.

Feasting.

The greatest gift is surrender. What you surrender to, you become.

Ascent Discovery Weekend,
seminar on victimhood

CHAPTER 19

The living room is filled with furniture that people with money and poor taste call Scandinavian. Every single lightbulb in this place is red. Everything is cast with a sickly, bloody glow.

"Come on," Emma says. "My car's—"

A maroon shadow with platinum blonde hair rushes out of the kitchen. There's a long kitchen knife in Arden's hand and a snarl on her face. She's panting hard. The slicked-down ponytail she had for the ritual is now a tangled mess falling in her eyes.

"Arden—"

"Shut up! You don't get to talk. You get eaten! You're the one it wants."

"It's starving," I say. "It wants everyone." I can *feel* its hunger now, even as it gorges.

"No, it's you! It wants you! *You're* the sacrifice!" Her voice is ragged with fear. "You're the one who's supposed to die. Not me! *I'm* supposed to be living my fucking truth, not trying to train some white-trash pity hire who can't even—!"

The French doors shatter. The god rolls onto the carpet in a hail of glass and fabric and wood.

Emma and I take advantage of the distraction to run past Arden toward the kitchen. We swing around the island, hands on the counter edge for balance.

Emma goes down hard ahead of me. She hits the tile floor with an awful fleshy slap. My feet tangle in hers and down I go too. Pain so strong that it momentarily steals my breath explodes in my knee.

Jena is huddled on the floor with her back against the island. Her hands are pressed to her mouth to keep any noise from escaping. She's what Emma tripped on.

"She's the one!" Arden yells. "She's the one you want!"

I get to my good knee and look over the island. The god is cast in red light and tall, so tall. Its head is tilted down so it doesn't hit the complicated chrome light fixture hanging from the ceiling. Arden motions with the knife toward the kitchen.

"She's over there!"

Jena yanks me down. This close, the smell of alcohol on her breath is overwhelming. It's hard to tell if it's the red light, or if her eyes are just that bloodshot.

Emma raises herself to her hands and knees. A red mark stands out on her temple. A blank look has overtaken her eyes.

Glass crunches under the god's feet with each step. Arden whimpers, then begins to sob. "It's not me, you stupid animal! I'm a good person! *She's* the sacrifice!"

A cut-off cry and then the blooming, overwhelming smell of blood and viscera fills the kitchen.

I point to the doorway and mime crawling. Emma blinks slowly. Jena shakes her head, tears pouring down her cheeks. I want to snap at her to stop it; that her tears mean nothing; that Arden would have doused Jena in gasoline and lit the match herself if she thought it'd keep her warm.

There's maybe ten feet between us and the doorway leading toward the front of the house. Emma starts the slow crawl. I bite the inside of my cheek against the pain in my knee. Even the smallest amount of pressure sets off stars behind my eyes.

Incredibly, Jena follows after us. Her face is resolute and her gaze straight ahead. Her lips quiver. No sound comes out, and though her nose is streaming snot she doesn't sniff or try to wipe it away.

The wet sound of the god eating itches across the back of my neck. A shiver of elation runs a finger down my spine. Every pause in the sound feels like if I look over my shoulder *it* will be looking back at me, hungry mouth wide.

Emma makes it into the hallway first. She helps me up when I cross the threshold. My breath catches when I try to put weight on my busted knee. I have to lean back on the wall and grind my teeth to stop the whimper from getting out. Jena's mostly able to stand on her own, which is fortunate because I am no help whatsoever and Emma is listing worryingly to the side.

The living room's minimalist style doesn't extend to the hallway. There's a long table pushed against the wall and a gaudy gold umbrella stand next to it. I take one out and use it as a cane. The muffled *tap, tap, tap* on the rug running down the hall makes my stomach twist with dread. The hallway opens into a white-and-black marble foyer with stairs leading to the second level tucked against the wall to my right.

Ripley's probably up there. In the video she was lying on a blanket, next to what looked like a footboard to a bed.

She can't still be alive, can she? She has to be gone with how ill she looked lying on that blanket.

But what if she's not?

What if she's not and she knows what's happening when the god sinks its teeth into her neck? What if the last thing she feels is fear and the last thing she sees is a room without me in it?

I'm eyeing the stairs trying to figure out if I could realistically make my way up them without Emma following me when there's a sound at the front door. The knob rotates but doesn't open.

"Unlock it," Jena whispers to Emma, who's the closest.

Emma shakes her head.

"Do it!" Jena repeats.

I turn to glare at her and tell her to shut up.

It's not Jena that my eyes fall on. It's the too-tall god

standing behind her—its chest expanding and contracting with sharp, silent breaths.

She sees the look on my face. "Wha—?"

The god's teeth are in her neck. Her face contorts. Blood stains the god's face. My broken brain hisses *Run*! and then Emma and I are running-stumbling-crawling up the stairs and I'm trying not to sob every time I jar my knee.

Three gunshots and the sound of the door splintering. The god makes a clicking, hissing scream. It's the sort of sound that belongs underground where the only witnesses are the earth and the rocks and ancient water.

Emma and I throw ourselves into the first room we see, then slam the door shut. More gunshots downstairs. Never in my life has a lock felt so useless. But what else can you do? What else can you do besides throw the lock that has no chance of keeping you safe, but might give you just one more second of life? You shove the dresser and shitty Ikea bookcase up against the door. That's what.

We've ended up in an impersonal guest room. Even the lightbulbs in here are red too.

There, lying on the floor, is Ripley.

What comes out of my mouth is supposed to be her name, but really, it's just a sob. I hobble over and use the bed's footboard to get on the ground with her. She's barely warm when I lay a hand on her ribs. And then she breathes. It's weak, but it's there.

I wish it wasn't.

I wish she'd slipped into death between one sleeping breath and another. I can't lift her, Emma can't lift her, and a ravenous god is going to tear through the door and eat all of us. I can't save her just like I couldn't save my mom. Just like I can't save myself.

I flinch when Emma puts her hand on my shoulder.

"Is she alive?"

I nod. Emma brushes her knuckles over Ripley's cheek, makes a quiet sound, then goes to look out the farthest window. A red glow takes up the bottom half of the window. The black of the night fills the rest. Smoke itches my nose and makes my eyes water.

"Can you see anything?"

Shadows cast sharp lines across Emma's profile. A bump is starting to form on her temple. She's shaking. "I don't know. There's too much smoke. There's a roof under the window, but it's still so high up."

"You have to jump." The moment I say it, I know it's true. "Do you have your keys?"

"What? No. I mean, the spare is in the hide-a-key, but I'm not gonna leave you. What's wrong with you?"

"Don't think we have time to go through that list." I try to smile. It doesn't work. She's mad. Furious. And then it drains away. She sits next to me. Her arm presses against mine.

"Sorry. I shouldn't have called you. Fuck. I'm sorry."

"I want to say it's not your fault, but it is. This would *not* have happened if your workplace was unionized."

That does make me laugh. Her breath gusts against my ear.

"I've put you through a lot over the last few months. I think I may have been insane? Or, like, maybe not insane, but not really interacting with reality either. Not an excuse but, ya know, there it is. Sorry."

"I appreciate that. It's not every day your best friend's mom dies, and then they literally never acknowledge it—not even at the funeral."

My stomach twists. I try to think of something to say. I can't. It's all so big and ugly. Instead, I let myself sit in this moment. I let myself feel the warm throb of the cut on the back of my head; the give of Emma's biceps pressing against mine; Ripley's soft fur and the curve of her ribs under my fingers. I can't save my dog, I couldn't save my mom, but maybe I can still save Emma. I have to at least try.

"We have to go," I say. "We can jump."

I use the umbrella to limp behind Emma to the window. It comes open easily. Smoke billows in to grease my cheeks and throat. The roof below is barely visible through the mixture of smoke and night. I don't know how many feet it is from here to there, but I do know Emma can make it. She was a skater kid up until junior year of high school. She knows how to fall. She knows how to get hurt and still be able to stand.

I bash the screen with the umbrella until it pops out to clatter on the shingles below.

"You first." She looks at me incredulously. "You have two working knees. Gonna need you to help me down."

Her face pinches, but she relents. Emma hoists a leg through the window. I keep my arm around her waist to steady her as she contorts herself to get her head and shoulders to the other side.

"Here. Hold on to this."

The umbrella is the ginormous golf kind that's longer than the window is wide. I brace it against the frame and hold it steady as she gets a firm grip.

The floor outside the room creaks. We both startle when something strikes the door.

Emma gets her leg over the frame and starts lowering herself. My hands hurt from how hard I'm holding the umbrella. What if it breaks and she falls hard enough to be paralyzed but not hard enough to die and she's conscious when the god eats her? What a terrible thought. What a horrible, terrible thought.

The god strikes the door again. The bookcase topples over.

"You have to jump," I say, my voice tight. "Like right now. You just have to do it. Right now!"

She inhales, then lets go. She hits the roof and rolls sideways, her body curved and handcuffed arms slapping the shingles. I knew she knew how to fall. I *knew* she could do it.

She smiles bright and surprised it worked, then immediately starts coughing. The smoke is so thick it looks like she's standing in brown fog.

"You next."

There are no words, so I don't say anything. I couldn't jump even if I wanted to. There's no way I could make it with my knee and the head wound and everything else. Even if I did I can't support myself, so Emma would do it like she's been doing for months. I know what it's like to feel so responsible for another person that you willingly and *gladly* carry their burdens on your back.

Emma's face crumples. "Don't."

I shake my head. I hope it translates: *I'm sorry, so fucking sorry you came here to help me and now I'm refusing to let you because you need to live and if I don't do this, you won't.*

Before I can shut the window, she yells, "Lou!" and smacks the side of the house. I lock the window—not that it'll do anything to stop a god but fuck I might as well—then pull the blinds down too just for good measure. I hope she shuts the fuck up and runs and runs and runs until she's safe.

I stand between the door and Ripley with my hand on the umbrella for balance. The door splinters and breaks until it's nothing more than a gaping hole. The god moves on the other side.

Time to die, the goblin says.

Time to die, I say back.

. . . reportedly consumed four of six mine ponies, one hauling mule, and thirteen men of various age and size. Such an appetite is a thing of rare occurrence. Rarer still is consumption with no elimination. The beast produces nothing. No waste, no sound, no tears.

. . . [the] animal may be struck repeatedly by a man with all his strength who is neither timid or fainthearted. There is no time even for it to bleed before its wounds heal.

I want to beg a favor of you, for which I know I can offer no apology. I have the greatest curiosity to continue observation of the beast. The quantity of new observations, profound and at times artful, has not yet begun to slow. Perhaps it is presumptuous of me to make a suggestion to a man of esteem such as yourself; but from what I have seen and have heard I have begun to suspect it is no beast at all.

Letter from Asa G. Witten to James Witten,
April 1906

CHAPTER 20

The god stoops through the hole. Its skin glistens and gleams with the sheer quantity of blood spilled tonight. One oily slick is different from the rest: black and thick and emanating from a raw hole the size of a softball in its chest.

The god's shoulders are curved inward, almost hunched. It's not doing anything at all other than standing and shaking. "Shuddering" might be a better word. Its lips tremble over its bloody teeth and its hands, fingers curled, shiver at its sides.

Ripley does the same shivery, shaking, wide-eyed focus thing when a squirrel darts across her path. "High drive," every trainer I've ever spoken to has told me. Her genes propel her to pursue prey until she can catch it in her jaws and shake.

The instinct is so . . . animal. Just like Arden called it.

For the first time since I saw it, I wonder: is the thing they've captured actually a god? Or just some ancient, unknowable predator they've managed to coerce? Is the prosperity Ellis talked about a result of this creature or is it just the vast store of generational wealth that keeps them thriving?

A figure steps into the room behind the god.

In one hand Ellis grips the gun. The other holds the whistle to his lips.

Ellis smiles wide and smug around the whistle, and then shoots me.

. . .

. . .

What?

That's the only thought my brain can produce when a force like a baseball bat smacks into the soft mound of my gut. It doesn't hurt. Mostly it just feels numb. I hear the gunshot. I see the gun. The two don't compute. It doesn't make sense.

What?

I make the mistake of looking down at my abdomen. Red. So much red—a river of it flows from the hole in my stomach onto the ugly white dress. The realization that I've been shot fills my head with a wave of dizziness that sends me to my knees. Landing on the injured one should have hurt, but I don't feel anything. Adrenaline floods my veins, then follows the rest of my blood as it leaves my body.

A burning, hot sensation like a throbbing infected molar chases away the numbness. The throbbing isn't just on my front, but at the small of my back too. Did it go all the way through? I reach around to touch, and yes. It did.

Ellis is talking. His mouth moves but his words are muffled.

He frowns, annoyed.

"I—"

—*was just* shot, *asshole*, I try to say, except I'm not sure I'm able to speak at all. Is this shock? Am I in shock?

"You think you *did* something with this?" Ellis waves the whistle to indicate the building around us. "Do you think you *changed* anything? 'House fire killed everyone on our leadership retreat. It's a tragedy. Donate to the GoFundMe. Attend our workshop on personal growth through grief.' We're gonna go viral! We'll get thousands at the next conference. All of them desperate for someone to tell them what to do. How to live a meaningful life. You did me a favor."

He coughs hard, then wipes at his eyes with the hand holding the whistle. It smears some of the blood from Emma cracking a pot on his skull. "I dropped the knife, so I can't do this the right way. It was ceremonial, but it was tradition."

He pulls one of the little black cicada stones from his pocket and tosses it at me. It hits my chest, bounces off my thigh, and lands in the blood pooling on the floor.

"What people don't understand is that tradition is *important*, and that ritual is *power*."

Before, he spoke with gravity. It almost felt holy. His words now are rushed and interspersed with coughing from the smoke.

"We offer this sacrifice—to you in supplication. May you deem us worthy—of your gifts in exchange." The god doesn't move, so Ellis gives two sharp whistles. "You're not coming back out for a while. Better eat up."

The god's nostrils flare. Its mouth twitches. I blink and suddenly the god is crouched on the floor. It's so long, so tall. A low chittering comes from the back of its throat. It's the sound a predator makes when it wants you to know it's there, lurking just out of sight.

I try to move away. Nothing's working right. Vertigo pushes me down till I'm on my back, looking up at a board-and-batten ceiling.

Ripley is only a few feet away. I hope she's gone. I hope if it eats her, she doesn't feel a thing.

The god lowers its head to the wound in my midsection. A searing pain makes the breath catch in my chest and a whine comes from my throat. I want to push it away. I want to smack this fucker in the face, but I can't *move*. With the blood loss and the chloroform and the head injury and and and so many ands—I can't do anything but take it.

I can't do anything

—but take it.

I'm so fucking tired. I'm so completely exhausted down to the marrow in my bones. Numbness is an ocean, and I've been submerged. Whatever it's doing at my midsection is no longer a priority. I can't muster the strength to look anywhere but the tacky paneled ceiling.

Eat me, I think, *so that I no longer have to breathe. Consume me so I don't have to carry the burden of thought. I want my head to be empty and the contents spilling onto the sheets. I just want to sleep.*

The ceiling is obscured by the face of the god. It hovers over me like a sleep-paralysis demon come to life. Red paints its chin and shines on its teeth. Rotting-meat smell overpowers the scent of smoke. A bullet had torn a path through its pectoral, leaving a cavity of raw meat behind. Ellis must have shot it after he busted through the front door. A glint of metal stands out from the exposed flesh. Behind it is something round and pulsing. Black ichor weeps from that wound and its mouth and all the injuries marking its body. It drips onto me, stinging the cracks on my lips and coating my tongue. I cough, but it only sends the liquid deeper down my throat.

I find enough strength to press my hand against its chest. Its skin is cold and quivering and it *hurts.* It *aches* all over. It's déjà vu again. It's the searing pain of skin meant to be kept in the dark being desiccated by the sun. It's a yawning pit of hunger that, no matter what's thrown into it, can't be filled. It's the consuming hatred for the things keeping you locked in a cage, alone and in an unnatural, ineffective dark.

I try to push the god and the sensations it's pouring into me away. Even when emaciated and dying, it's immovable.

And it *is* dying.

Or maybe I'm confusing the feeling of my own death with the god's.

I think it's both.

I mean, why not, right? Why not die in the same way I've lived? Why not let this god eat through all my vital parts? Not that there's much left. It's the end of the feast; only the dregs remain.

Your parents were alcoholics who resented you? Here's a kidney, Mom. Hope that helps.

You're so happy for me to be part of the incoming freshman class, but there's no money left for scholarships? No worries, here's my pinkie finger lobbed off with a butcher knife. Surely this will taste good going down.

You worked sixty hours but we still can't pay the electricity bill? I'm twelve and not sure how to fix the hurt in your voice, so I cut out a chunk of thigh meat for you to eat. Is this a comfort? Do you want more?

The answer was always yes. Whether it was my student loan provider, or the manager at the Taco Bell where I worked third shift, or my mom drowning me in her trauma and filling me up with her hopes, they all wanted more more more.

Now this thing wants to eat me too. And just like with everyone and everything else, eating me won't do any good because *I'm* not the one killing it.

Ellis coughs hard. He's hidden by the god's bulk, but his voice is clear. "Come on!"

The god grimaces, and suddenly I'm sure this thing hovering over me with my blood painted across its mouth isn't a god. It has the capacity for disdain, so it's not an animal either. It's something *Other.*

Whatever it is, it's opening its mouth wide. It strikes, latching onto the place where my neck and shoulder meet. Its mouth is a vise made of broken glass. Something snaps. I think my collarbone.

I take a wheezing breath—maybe the last one I ever will—and bore my fingers into the greasy wound in its chest. There's a bullet buried in the slowly pulsing heart there. Still, it beats. It's so strange that something so Other can have the same thing in its chest that I do.

I dig my nails into yielding flesh and pull. What comes out is one special thing: its heart.

The first step to changing the world is committing to change yourself. Unlike the cicada, you are not alone in pulling yourself from the earth. We raise you up, then crack you open and uproot every limiting belief clogging your soul. What's left is the beginning of the rest of your life.

Ascent Initiation Script

CHAPTER 21

I'm so tired of being eaten. I'm so tired of handing over pieces of myself so that someone else can fill their mouths in the vain hope of being satiated.

Can't say I don't understand though.

Because now, with my mouth slick with blood and raw meat sliding down my throat, I get it. The god's flesh is a summer ripe peach between my teeth.

It feels *good* to eat.

Black blood pours from its chest with every fistful I pull out. The smell of deep earth and sweet decay fill the room until I'm swimming in it.

It—the god, the thing, the monster—spasms, but doesn't move away. It doesn't even let go of where it has me in its teeth. I feel its surprise like it's my own. There's something else there too, but it doesn't matter. All that matters is filling my mouth.

Ellis is yelling. That doesn't matter either.

There's a gunshot and then another. Both hit the body above me. It shrieks and grows heavier, but still it stays.

I plunge my hand in up to my wrist and pull out more meat to put in my mouth. There's a black hole in my gut. I've thrown in bits and pieces here and there, but nothing came close to filling it up. Howling hunger rips through me until all I am is gnashing teeth and a throat swallowing.

There's running feet and coughing. Is Ellis gone? I don't care. I don't care because I've been hungry my whole life, and now I can finally eat. It's finally my turn to feast, to take bites out of something alive, just like how living in this world and for someone else took never-ending bites out of me.

Finally, the god pulls away. I follow, fingers hooked in the sharp angles of its shoulders.

There's blood in my eyes, in my nose, drenching my skin. The wound at my stomach glows coal-hot. My jaw stretches until it threatens to come undone, and then it does. It might hurt. It might feel like something. Mostly it makes it easier to push hunks of meat down my throat to the cavern below.

The god chokes and shakes while I gorge myself on more and more and more. I burrow my arm down its throat. Its tongue comes away easy and comes apart in my mouth like butter.

Eventually, it's still and I'm left panting.

Buzzing insects stuff my skull with white noise. I didn't know it was possible to feel like this—so full and filled up and *warm*.

A twitch wracks my body. And another and another and now I'm on my hands and knees. Bile and meat spray out of my mouth. Pressure builds up behind my eyes, making my vision go red as my blood vessels pop pop pop. Convulsions grip my arms and my legs. My fingers twist in the blood-soaked blanket spread out under Ripley.

Every nerve ending is a shining beacon of pain. In the movies, characters pass out when they're faced with insurmountable pain. They squirm and shriek but eventually fall quiet to blessed unconsciousness. The pain no longer pains them; the horror no longer horrifies them; they are allowed to rest.

There is no rest, and the horror does not stop no matter how I beg.

This isn't what I wanted.

Except it is, isn't it? It's exactly what I wanted: to take back every pound of my flesh that's been consumed by others till I'm so full, I'll never be empty again.

CHAPTER 22

The world is red, swirling, and thick.

I am in a room, on the floor, twisted in a blanket. I flex my jaw since it's now back in its socket. The taste of carbon and earth coats my tongue and the insides of my cheeks.

The decimated body of a god lies next to me. Its blood has formed a lake as shining and thick as oil on the floor.

Ripley is curled on her side in the puddle. She's frozen in time on her last breath. Mouth slightly ajar, her gums are a pale pink that stands out against the sea of black. It almost feels like she's only sleeping when I cup her cheek. She can't stay here. Even if she's gone, I have to get her out. I go to scoop her up—

A sharp pain rips through my chest, like my ribs are doing their damnedest to break through the cage of my skin—like there's something in there trying to get out. My legs crumple like rotten wood and spill my limbs onto the floor when I try to stand.

A hysterical sound comes out of my mouth. It's a laugh. Why is it funny? I don't know, but it is.

"Hello? Help!" A faint voice comes from down the hall. The words are followed by rasping, heaving coughs.

The world narrows to a point, and saliva fills my mouth. A vague humming shakes the space between my ears. The humming spreads to my eyes, then down my throat, across my stomach, until the entirety of my body is zinging with trapped energy. An achy fever settles in the hinge of my jawbone. Clenching my teeth and grinding my molars does nothing to dispel the feeling.

I follow the sound and find a cultist crawling through the doorway of one of the other bedrooms. I can smell her—the salt of her sweat, the iron tang of her blood, the astringent chemical scent of the product in her hair. I breathe quick and fast to get more of it in my nose and on the back of my tongue. It's good. It's *good.*

She doesn't notice she's not alone until her hand bumps my bare foot. A strangled noise of surprise breaks up the steady coughs contracting her lungs.

"Oh my God! Can you help me? Oh my God, please. He left. He left us!"

It takes her panic-flushed skin on mine to realize how cold this body is and how desperately it needs to be filled with something warm.

The cultist looks up. What she sees wipes the mask of desperation from her face and replaces it with the sort of fear that lingers in the primal, hidden parts of a body.

She's on her back and I'm on her. The skin of her neck splits around my teeth. Her honeybee earrings tangle in my hair. There's blood dripping down my chin; blood on my hands; a chanting in my head that I embrace like a missing friend.

I find a cultist shuffling down the stairs through the ocean of smoke. I crack his neck like a twig and taste the ropey muscles of his back. Another limps through the foyer toward the front door. It's the tall woman with the willow-thin wrists.

She holds up the crosshair. "Get back!"

A hiss like a startled cat comes out of my mouth. Even the sight of it is repellent.

But I don't have to look at it to take her to the ground. The rune goes flying. A puff of hot, terrified breath hits my cheek. I have the urge to eat it directly from her lungs, so I do.

She shouldn't have tried to hurt me. She shouldn't have tried to hurt Emma or Ripley. None of them should have.

They deserve it, the goblin says.

Except, there never was a goblin, was there? It was just me. The goblin was the voice I gave to the destructive urges and intrusive thoughts that kept me up at night. People give names to the things that scare them all the time. I'm no different.

The thing inside urging me to *eat them hurt them break them* bite?

That's not me. Not the goblin either.

Outside, I tilt my face up to the moon. Nothing like the

sky out here. These mountains might be older than bones, but not older than the stars. I touch my cheeks and trace the unexpected upward tilt of my lips. It feels good to smile.

A figure rushes through the front yard toward the driveway. Cars have filled it up since I was out here. The figure lurches toward the last one in the line. A set of keys jangle in his hand.

Ellis freezes with one hand on the car. Fear sounds like him swallowing with a dry mouth and smells like ammonia leaking from his pores.

The fever in my jawbone throbs. The sores from the box burn. He locked me in and took me out to brag, for meaningless ceremony, to bless his small life, and to never, not once, be satiated—

I shake my head and press both hands to my chest. The pressure inside builds and builds. My bones are going to crack and my flesh is going to split. Outside, nothing happens. No splitting, no breaking. Inside, it's so *crowded.*

"That you in there, Lou?" Ellis calls. "Looks like you, but I think it's the god."

It is me.

But there might be something else too.

The car's headlights flash. He gets the door halfway open. One kick and the handle tears out of his hand. Shattered glass rains onto the gravel from the window.

Ellis runs down the driveway onto the road. I let him.

His heart is a rabbit's back feet kicking frantic against a predator's chest. He's quick, but not quick enough. I jump on his back. We fall together. He twists, sends an elbow to my chin. It doesn't hurt, doesn't feel like anything. The only thing I can feel is the warmth of his body below mine—the only thing I can think of is how good that warmth is going to be in my stomach.

"Lou, Lou, please! You don't need to do this! You can fight it! You're better than this!"

Strands of hair stick to his cheeks. Every visible expanse of skin is coated in a sheen of sweat. His eyes are open wide like if he can see enough of the world, he'll be okay.

"I'm really not."

His ribs might as well be hollow for how willingly they break in my hands. The expanse within, a feast.

CHAPTER 23

Cicadas fill the night with a constant, reverberating buzz.

They land on my skin and tangle in my hair. The white bones sticking up like headstones in the cemetery of Ellis's chest are covered with them. I'd draw this scene with black ink. Hatch marks for shading. Negative space. Red pen for the cicadas, I think.

The forest rustles just beyond the tree line.

Ripley steps onto the road. Her tail is up, her head low between her shoulders, and her ears back. There's a tension to her body—a question to her stance—like she can't figure out whether to bare her teeth or run. She looks at me and I look at her.

"Ripley? Here."

Her ears twitch out of sync. First one and then the other, like she's trying to figure out where the sound she just heard came from. A beat. Another. And then she shakes off the tension and trots over to me.

She puts her paws on my thighs and sticks her nose in my

ear. Every inch of her coat is drenched in god's blood. That's what did this. It has to be. It made a rotting coyote chase me, a dead raccoon wink, and fixed the mangled hole punched through my gut. Repairing some internal damage from getting hit by a car doesn't seem so wild in comparison.

I pull her close and let myself be happy she's alive, even if she's not as warm as she used to be.

Headlights wash over us. They make a shadowed mountain of the body splayed out on the road. My vision blazes white and spotty. The car stops and sits with the engine running. The headlights make it impossible to see who's inside. The occupant's heart isn't quite the rabbit beat of Ellis's. It's not slow either.

The driver doesn't budge when I get to the passenger side and peer through the window at her silhouette.

Without looking at me, Emma unlocks the car.

Ripley jumps in and settles herself in the back seat when I open the passenger-side door. It closes with a soft *whumpf.* Can't hear the cicadas in here. Can't hear the forest or taste the muggy heat of the night. It's just me, Emma, Ripley, the smell of Emma's fear, and the sound of her handcuffs clinking around her shaking hands.

Emma grips the steering wheel. Her knuckles are white. Would her flesh be bloodless if I bit it now? I don't want to find out. I won't let myself find out.

Next to me, Emma opens her mouth, closes it. She looks at me with wide, manic eyes, then turns to stare out of the windshield again.

"I'd write Ellis my resignation. But I ate him."

Her laugh comes out wet and frantic. She puts her face into her hands and rests her forehead on the steering wheel.

"Sorry for dragging you into this."

"Yeah. Thanks. Hey, quick question. Wasn't Ripley pretty much dead last time I saw her?"

Ripley pops up in the back seat at the sound of her name, panting softly and tongue lolling. We both stare at her in the rearview mirror.

I shrug. I might not know what happened, but I know she's my dog.

The satisfaction of consuming Ellis is starting to fade. He's disintegrating inside of me, becoming part of my flesh, my bones, the collagen in my nails. I want more. I want as much as I can possibly get. I want to eat and be full.

"I'm hungry."

"Well." Emma breathes in deep, then lets it out slow. She puts the car into drive. "Let's find you something to eat."

ACKNOWLEDGMENTS

Thank you a thousand times over to Susan Graham for diligently shepherding me through *so many* manuscripts, edits, submissions, revisions, life changes, etc. You are a tenacious and extremely adept literary agent and a true friend. I'm very glad to know you.

To my editor, Kristin Temple, thank you for the considerable attention and care you put in to shaping Lou's story. I'm forever grateful that this story ended up in your extremely capable hands. A massive thanks to the whole Tor Nightfire team: Heather Saunders, Jess Kiley, Rafal Gibek, Jessica Katz, Jacqueline Huber-Rodriguez, Jordan Hanley, Michael Dudding, Valeria Castorena, and Laura Etzkorn. I have been continuously impressed by the depth of your creativity and expertise at every step of this process.

Thank you to Olivia for being the best friend and best person I think I'll ever know; Mike, Ann, and Regina for giving me the language to think and talk about the craft of writing; CJ for your firearm expertise; to every café I've ever written in but specifically Index Coffee & Books, Java Central, and Phoenix Coffee; lastly, to my mom, thank you for every trip to the bookstore (even when we couldn't afford it) and reading my first drafts (even when they were horrible). The first step on the path that led me here was you repeatedly telling middle school me that I could.

ABOUT THE AUTHOR

Carter Keane resides in and is inspired by the frequently odd and often horrifying state of Ohio. Keane writes books where the monster and the monstrous, in the end, are not the same. *Morsel* is their debut.

carterkeane.com